THE FORGOTTEN ISLAND

THE
FORGOTTEN
ISLAND

a novel

SASHA TROYAN

A
TIN HOUSE
BLOOMSBURY
BOOK

A Tin House/Bloomsbury Book

Published by Bloomsbury, New York and London
Distributed to the trade by Holtzbrinck Publishers

Library of Congress Cataloging-in-Publication Data

Troyan, Sasha, 1962–
The forgotten island : a novel / Sasha Troyan. – 1st U.S. ed.
p. cm.
ISBN 1–58234–464–7
1. Girls – Fiction. 2. Islands – Fiction. 3. Sisters – Fiction.
4. Summer resorts – Fiction. 5. Missing persons – Fiction.
6. Mediterranean Area – Fiction. I. Title.

PS3620.R69F67 2004
813'.6 – dc22
2003025552

First U.S. Edition 2004

1 3 5 7 9 10 8 6 4 2

Typeset by Hewer Text Ltd, Edinburgh
Printed in the USA by
Quebecor World Fairfield

THE FORGOTTEN ISLAND

1

Every summer, we returned to Bella Terra, an island off the coast of Italy swept by winds: the cool mistral from the north, or the hot sirocco from Africa. According to an ancient legend, the wind was born on the island. The water was so clean you could see from the plane right through to the white sand. My parents built a villa on the side of a hill. Painted ocher, the same color as the rock out of which it had been carved, the villa would have blended completely into the hillside had it not been for the brilliant purple bougainvillea covering its roof, the streams of *amanti del sole* and white gardenias that ran from the veranda to the stone wall at the bottom of the garden.

Our villa overlooked the sea on both sides; on one side you could see, far into the distance, islands, beyond that the sea merged into the sky; on the other, a golf course, which dipped and ran all the way to the Piccolo Pevero's turquoise water, where my sister, Lea, and I had learned to swim. The golf course was so green it seemed incongruous on an island that was mostly dry and brown, covered with bushes and rocks. There were very few trees, mostly cypress; only the gardens of the rich and the hotels could afford sprinklers.

Each year we found the island hardly changed. A consortium regulated the number of villas and hotels constructed, stipulating even their color and their height.

The last summer we returned, everything was exactly as we remembered it, except a superhighway now circumvented the small industrial port of Dolia. We were transported above shores, narrow streets with shuttered houses.

As a child, I was disappointed not to catch a glimpse of the immense ships, the clothes hanging on lines, but glad to have our journey shortened. The journey from the airport to the villa had always seemed too long.

The day we arrived, the island was enveloped in mist. The taxi driver bemoaned our luck. They had had two weeks straight of perfect weather. "Sole senza vento," he said. "Sun without wind." He joked that we were responsible. He turned to stare at Mother. "You're not Italian," he said. "Una straniera. Like Catherine Deneuve. French." He must have read the labels of the suitcases. Lea and I had insisted on writing, "M. et Mme. Dashley, 28 Rue Guynemer, Paris 75006, France."

"No," Father said, answering for Mother. "She's South African."

From the moment the cabdriver said "You an American?" implying by his question that Father's accent in Italian was too perfect for him to be an American, Father had taken a liking to him. I did not like the thin stubble of hair covering the cabdriver's bony head nor his synthetic blue shirt with pink bunny rabbits.

Mother had not wanted Father to take this cab, and like her I could not understand why he had chosen it. It was much smaller than the other cabs, and the back windows would not open. I sat squeezed between Lea and Mother, who held on to the driver's seat. Despite the long journey, her shirt was without crease, her blond hair pulled into a smooth bun. Father sat in the front because of his long legs. His head almost touched the roof of the car and each time we went over a bump I wondered if he was going to hit it.

"Expensive camera," the cabdriver remarked, referring to Father's Leica. "Are you a photo—"

"No, I'm—" Father said.

"Let me guess," he said. "In the movie business—"

"Magazine, I'm afraid," Father said.

"A reporter?"

"No, I'm the publisher."

"Just as well. They don't like reporters on the island."

"Why not?" Father asked.

"So many famous people. Only the rich vacation on the Costa Paradiso."

"Well, we're not famous," Mother said.

The cabdriver winked at Mother in the rearview mirror as if to say that he did not believe her. Mother had to be some famous actress or singer in disguise.

She was wearing a brown linen suit that set off her blond hair, white sandals with thick rubber soles. "All you need is a little nurse's cap to go with those shoes," Father had said that morning. Even at eleven, I could see he was right, but I thought Mother beautiful no matter what she wore. Now I'm tempted to believe that Mother's lapses in taste, as Father used to call them, were

3

deliberate. She almost always sabotaged the effect of her elegant attire by wearing something incongruous.

It's doubtful that the cabdriver perceived this lapse. "Like sisters," he said.

I flushed with pleasure, thinking, for a moment, he meant Lea and me, but then realized that he was referring to Lea and Mother.

Lea did not respond. She kept her cheek pressed to the dirty window. She was wearing the expensive sunglasses Father had bought her. They were adult glasses, in fashion in the early 1970s, with black rims, a silver crescent at each corner. The dark brown lenses dwarfed her face, making her look like a dragonfly.

Mother reached into her brown leather bag with the wood knob then whispered that she must have left her sunglasses on the counter of the bar at the airport when she and Father had had espressos, not to tell Father.

Father reached to untangle a wooden cross from photographs of women that dangled from the rearview mirror.

"My wife and daughters," the cabdriver said.

"Sure."

"Sì, sì, sì," the driver said and laughed. "The others—" He reached into his pocket. I caught only a glimpse of his wallet as it unfolded to reveal an array of pictures of women. "Ah e donne!"

"Ah yes, e donne!" Father said, glancing teasingly in the rearview mirror to catch Mother's eye.

Mother did not laugh. She squeezed my wrist tighter. She muttered something in French about Italian drivers. "How can he pass that car?" she asked. "He cannot see what is around the bend. Please, tell him to keep his eyes on the road."

"Why don't you tell him yourself?" Father said.

"I saw la più bella donna 'sta mattina," the driver went on. "Quasi beautiful as la signora, blond too. The most—" And here he took his hands off the wheel to demonstrate the size of her breasts. Father laughed uneasily, then leaned forward and turned on the radio, which came on crackling. At the same time, he muttered something to the driver, who said, "Scusi, scusi," nodding toward the back of the car. Beyond the next hill, the radio would work better, he assured Father. The cabdriver's movements were jerky, even the way he drove the car, slamming on the brakes then speeding up.

I started to feel light-headed, queasy. My forehead broke into a sweat. The highway had graduated all too soon to a narrow road where you were not supposed to pass other cars but where everyone did. It consisted mostly of sharp turns, around steep mountains, over narrow passes. The sheer drops to the sea were dizzying. The fact that we could not roll down the windows in the back added to my discomfort. The air was oppressive, despite the gray sky.

"I'm feeling sick," I whispered to Mother.

"Can you open the window?" Mother asked Father. He rolled it down an inch. Now he could not hear the radio. And when at last it was working, he rolled up the window again.

I whispered again, "I'm going to be sick."

He rolled it down an inch, but soon enough rolled it up again. He and the cabdriver were completely engrossed with the game on the radio. Father rooted for the French not because he really cared that they win but just to annoy the driver. Mother was for the Italians because she always rooted for the losing team.

I kept breathing loudly, swallowing my saliva. It was Lea who at last shouted at Father, "She's going to throw up if you don't stop."

The car came to a sudden halt on the side of a cliff. I clambered out after Mother. I threw up on a dry bush. She stood by, pulling her jacket around herself. Her eyes were focused on the horizon. But there was no one. Just the cliff and the sea. I took her hand, knowing that she was upset with Father.

When I got back into the car, Lea still sat with her face pressed to the window. She was detached from the conversation. Our parents had been fighting ever since we had left our house in Paris. They had fought in the car on the way to the airport because Father had arrived late. They fought at the airport when Father realized that Mother had forgotten the small attaché case he had reminded her three times to bring. They fought on the airplane because Mother had not thought to specify seats on the plane and as a result they were in the smoking section by the kitchen, where Mother was more inconvenienced because she was not a smoker but where Father complained because he was being bumped by the air hostess every time she passed. Mother had offered her seat but Father had to be on the aisle because of his long legs. Mother had even offered to have me move to her side, but by then we were no longer allowed to move from our seats. The only respite from their fighting came when the plane was buffeted by the wind. Drinks were spilled. Ice cubes dropped down the shirt of the woman across the aisle from us. Lea was the only one to have fun. She enjoyed the sudden drops, the sudden hikes, people's cries. "It's like a roller coaster," she said. I sat as still as I could, my fingers resting on the sick bag.

Now, in the car, Lea did not laugh at being thrown against me as we turned round a bend. From time to time she would glance at the tiny gold wristwatch Father had just given her for her thirteenth birthday, or she would point out a rock formation she thought she recognized from the summer before. "Look, there's the falcon rock," she called out. "The hat. The giant." There was not much for her to recognize. We were unfamiliar with this part of the island. We hardly ventured beyond the small enclave surrounding our villa.

The cabdriver pointed out a nuraghe. Lea said she saw it and then Father did. I did not know what to look for. All I could see were pastures cut by stone walls, sheep gathered in circles beneath bushes. From the pastures, we passed suddenly around a corner into a blackened area, where some trees were reduced to stumps while others retained only a few branches that stretched like withered arms toward the sky. The smell of burned wood pervaded the air. The cabdriver told us that there had been a terrible fire. A whole family died trapped in their car.

"What is a nuraghe?" I said. "I can't—"

"Shush," Mother said, as the driver took one hand off the wheel to point in the direction of the nuraghe. "We'll all be killed. It's just a tower. There're thousands like it on the island."

I wanted to know what the nuraghi were for, but Mother, who

7

was studying art history, said that even the archaeologists were not sure. Some kind of tomb built out of stone without mortar. I did not know what mortar meant either, and Mother had to explain. Lea wanted to stop by the next nuraghe we passed.

"Just for a second," she begged.

Mother did not want to. There was no place to stop, a car might round the curve.

"It's dangerous," Mother said, and Father said, "Now don't you pick on my favorite." He liked to tease us in this way; alternately calling me his favorite then Lea. She shrugged, the back of her dress unbuttoning, revealing the bathing suit she wore underneath.

I recall Lea's dress. It was purple with mutton sleeves edged with white, the bodice closely gathered with bright red thread.

Later, Mother would insist that Lea was wearing the purple dress the day she disappeared. But the police found it hanging in the closet along with the clothes everyone else had said she was wearing. Father swore she wore a bathing suit and towel. Mrs. Ashton, a blue and white sailor suit. Mr. Ashton said that he did not notice that sort of thing. I can still hear the police saying, over and over again, "Nessuno sa," nobody knows, in an accusatory tone.

They did not ask me. If they had, I would have told them that she wore a white dress, no shoes—just a white towel dress, with a matching bikini. She complained the bottom piece was too tight around the legs and the waist. I remember her lifting up the skirt of the dress to show me the red marks. It was one of my favorite dresses. I was eleven years old at the time, Lea thirteen.

*   *   *

8

A rainbow hung over the arch leading to the villa, the slab of granite where the name of our villa should have been inscribed still blank. Mother and Father could not agree on a name. Mother wanted to call it Crossways after the house her family had owned when she was a child, while Father wanted to give it an Italian name, L'Avventura. The cabdriver insisted on carrying our suitcases. Despite his small frame, he carried two suitcases in each hand. He complimented Father on the villa, saying he had never seen the like. And he knew almost all the villas in that area. Take the one beneath ours, Mr. Peters's villa, a complete wreck—not surprising since everyone knew that he was . . . the cabdriver pointed to his head. And the one on the other side, which belonged to the famous writer, nice, but the windows were too narrow, the garden not landscaped. Now our villa was perfect; the only thing missing, a swimming pool. If Father needed someone to build a pool, he knew just the man. Even after Father had paid him, tipping, as he always did, exorbitantly, the cabdriver lingered, peering into the living room, as if he wished Father would offer to give him a tour. He left only after he had mopped his forehead several times with the sleeve of his shirt.

Father was very proud of the villa, which he had designed with the help of a famous architect from the island, particularly proud of the landscaped garden built on a slope. He insisted on inspecting it. Lea wanted to go down to the beach immediately. "You promised," she said, smiling up at Father, holding the bridge of her glasses with one finger.

"It'll just take a few minutes," he said. "Look at the lemon tree."

"But it's sunny now," she said.

"Don't whine."

He took Lea by the arm but she broke away, running ahead, disappearing down the steep path. I lingered with Mother by the hydrangeas, while Father walked on, swinging his head from side to side. Mother explained that in order for the hydrangeas to be blue the soil had to be acidic.

The garden was redolent with the scent of oleander, juniper, and lavender. It had never been as luxuriant. Pine trees had shot up several feet. Vines now shaded the veranda completely. Kumquats, gardenias, blue plumbago, verbena, *amanti del sole* grew in profusion, overriding the carefully planned flower beds.

All summer I mistook the verbena for the *amanti del sole*, thinking that the name, lovers of the sun, must be coupled with the beautiful tiny red and orange flowers, when, in fact, the *amanti del sole* were purple flowers with waxy green leaves that overhung walls.

The sun slipped in and out of the clouds, the garden changing moment to moment from black-and-white to color. Mother said what a shame that so many lemons had gone bad. She was reaching to pick one that seemed about to drop, the branch bending under the fruit's weight, when Lea emerged from the bushes, startling us.

"I wish you wouldn't do that," Mother said. Behind one ear Lea had placed a flaming red hibiscus. She pulled me by the arm and we ran down the path, past Father, all the way to the wall at the bottom of the garden where eucalyptus trees gave off a strange odor.

She ducked behind a bush. "Let's go down to the beach," she said.

"But we'll get into trouble," I said, hesitantly, knowing this was not what she wanted to hear.

"You're such a bore," she said, in the cynical tone she had recently adopted with me.

"I'm not a bore."

"You are."

She pushed me against a bush. The hard leaves scratched my arm. I pushed her back.

Just then we heard our parents' voices. We crouched down, knees touching.

"How could you?" Mother said.

"He really did go too far—" and then Father laughed. He imitated the cabby cupping his hands to demonstrate the size of the woman's breasts.

"It's not that, although that was in very poor taste," she said. "You know what I'm referring to."

"No, I don't. What are you talking about? Just come out with it."

"If you're going to lie about it now—"

"Oh fuck," he said. "Don't be ridiculous—"

Mother turned and ran up the steps. We waited for the sound of their footsteps to die before climbing up the hill, not along the path but through the pine trees and oaks. In some places the trees were so densely packed there was no light. The ground was covered with brown pine needles, which crunched beneath our feet. Several times I slipped and almost lost my balance, regaining it at the last minute by clinging to a branch, or the trunk of a tree.

At the villa, Lea told me to pick out the pine needles from her socks. I bent over and tried to extract each pine needle. But some were so deeply embedded they were hard to remove and Lea grew tired of standing and flopped down on the couch. In the end, she simply leaned over and pulled off her socks, leaving them in the middle of the living room. She sent me for our straw baskets, snorkels, and masks. We were already wearing our bathing suits. All we had to do was pull off our dresses. Still our parents did not emerge from their room. We pressed our ears to their door. We could not hear a sound, so we roamed through the villa, revisiting each room.

As a child I liked the colors of the villa: the white walls, the glazed terra-cotta tiles, the kitchen tiles with their pattern of blue boats. The tile felt cool beneath our feet. The house smelled slightly musty after remaining closed for so many months. Most of the furniture, the desks, even the base of the sofa, were carved out of the rock of the island, immovable. The rest was constructed of wood and painted a light blue: blue chairs and blue bed frames and blue bedside tables decorated the rooms. I particularly liked the light fixtures, mother-of-pearl shells, larger than any I had found in the sea, glass lamps filled with tiny pink shells.

In retrospect, I see the villa differently. On the one hand, it seemed very private; each bedroom had its own bathroom, its own patio with potted geraniums, thick walls. On the other hand, because the villa was mostly glass, it now seems to me exposed and vulnerable. It was also highly impractical, but that too, I realize only now. I remember the caretaker, Adriana, cleaning the glass doors and the white tiles in the bathrooms and kitchen. The bathtubs were so immense we could not fill them. The water supply was limited and the water pressure was never very good so that the best you could hope for from the showers was a steady trickle.

Finally, Lea grew impatient and knocked on our parents' door, announcing, "We're going down to the beach." At this point, though I would not have taken the initiative, I felt her action was justified. We flew out the house, down a paved road that twisted and turned, over a wood gate, and onto a dirt road where the scent of myrtle and rosemary and lavender, *macchia* they called it, pervaded the air.

We stopped only once to peer down an overgrown alley, through a mass of brambles, at Mr. Peters's villa, the same villa the cabdriver had referred to earlier as a wreck. It seemed even more neglected than the summer before, crumbling beneath a mass of vines and bougainvillea. The paint peeled off the shutters. The garden was overgrown, littered with paintings. Several canvases were torn, branches growing through them.

We paused only for a moment, eager to plunge into the water. "I'll race you to the beach," Lea said, setting off. I ran as fast as I could, but she was faster. She ran and ran. Then all of a sudden she stopped. We were about halfway down the road. "They're trespassing," she said, pointing to people in the distance. "They must be punished." She handed me a stick. We crept up. My cheeks were burning. I did not believe I could do it. One woman with bright red lipstick smiled at us. Lea whipped out her stick, hitting the lady's behind. I whipped out the stick from behind my back and hit her bum. She screamed. We ran and ran, laughing. We did not turn back until we had emerged, beyond the green golf course, a few feet from the Piccolo Pevero beach.

Lea laughed again because I would not take off my towel. I wanted to drop it by the edge of the water. She ran across the beach and jumped into the sea, holding her knees at the last minute, like a bomb we used to call it. We could see on the horizon a motorboat pulling a water-skier. The water-skier zipped back and forth over the waves. At first we swam in the bay, where the water was shallow. I held on to Lea's waist, kicking my legs while she breaststroked. I pretended we were one person. She was the arms, I was the legs. Then I floated onto my back in Lea's wake, feeling the pulse of her kicks, still connected, until she outdistanced me.

We swam beyond the clear blue water to shadowy areas where I had never ventured, searching for sea urchin shells. We could not resist collecting shells even though we knew that after only a few minutes outside the water they would lose their color, becoming pale reflections of themselves. The shells came mostly in green and pink. I can still see Lea turning round underwater, waving for me to follow, her face strange and white behind her mask, her lips distorted by the snorkel.

She had spotted a purple shell, eight or nine feet below the surface, between two rocks covered with live sea urchins. Lea dove first but missed the shell. I did not want to dive. I was afraid of brushing against the live sea urchins. "Go on," she said, treading water, "I dare you."

I took a deep breath and dove. The water became progressively colder and darker. I could not see the shell: just rocks and seaweed, then a frond of dark seaweed moved back like a hand and I caught sight of the shell. I hesitated, but I could feel Lea gazing down at me. I reached out, trying to avoid touching the seaweed, visualizing the sea urchins' black spines catching on my hand. Gently, I lifted out the shell, holding my hand half-open because the shells crumbled so easily.

By then I was out of breath and kicked furiously to get back up to the surface. In my haste, I must have opened my hand too wide. The shell floated out of my grasp, wobbled, and then dropped, landing a few feet farther into the reef. Lea said she would try again, but I begged her not to. I wanted to return to shore.

I watched her dive for it, her fuchsia bathing suit fluorescent against the black water. She reached it easily and turned to look at me before coming up to the surface. I knew she was thinking, "See, it's easy." Instead of returning to the beach, she swam out farther. I called after her, but she either didn't hear me or had decided she was going to go on no matter what. I did not want to return alone. I treaded water for a time, then decided to return to shore since she was already so far from me.

The return journey seemed to take much longer; one cove led into another and yet another. I kept turning to see if Lea was following. I didn't like the black water. I couldn't even see my legs. I kept my eyes glued to the turquoise water sparkling ahead. Now and again I felt something brush against me. I saw a dark shape and remembered Lea telling me that sharks went for you if you panicked. They were attracted to blood. There were no sharks off Bella Terra, but a few years before two had got lost and found themselves in the port of Dolia. Several times I had to hold myself back from screaming, from flailing my arms and legs about.

When I reached the clear water, I saw that Lea had somehow contrived to get to the beach before I did. She must have walked part of the way, cutting across land, swimming just the last stretch.

She stood with her back to the beach, carefully removing the shell from inside the bottom piece of her bathing suit. She was just starting to get a thin down of golden hair, which she liked to show off to me. She was also getting breasts, which she had let me touch once. I called them "lumps" to annoy her and because that was what they felt like to me.

I did not follow her as she skipped across the beach to where our father now lay alone. There was no sign of Mother. I busied myself by emptying the sand from my bathing suit. Out of the corner of my eye, however, I observed her. A few feet from Father, Lea shouted, "Daddy, look, I found a purple shell." Father did not move. He appeared to have fallen asleep in the sun. He had forgotten his umbrella and his back was already pink. It was one of those strange quirks of nature that Father and I should be so dark and burn so easily, while Mother and Lea were so blond and could lie in the sun with impunity. Lea tiptoed up to Father. She leaned over him then twisted her long hair so that drops of water fell onto his back. He leapt up, shouting, "Don't you do that." He tried to grab at her legs, but she ran away laughing, kicking up sand as she raced across the beach toward me.

I returned to my task. I could not get the sand out from my

bathing suit completely. I even had sand in my hair. I could feel it in my scalp.

"Don't you want to see it?" she asked. I shook my head.

"Go on," she said. "Very well."

When I turned round, she had disappeared. The purple shell lay in pieces on the sand. I knelt and tried to reconstruct it, but it was impossible, and after arranging the pieces in the form of a boat, I wandered over the dunes where the sand was fine and soft. Here and there nettles grew, but they were bright yellow and easy to spot.

2

The next morning we were sitting around the breakfast table. There was no proper dining room, but a dining area that continued off the living room. You had only to go up a few steps. From this elevated position, you could see the garden, beyond it the golf course, and in the distance the sea. Still in our nightdresses, Lea and I had just finished eating our toast. Mother had sat down at the same time as we had, but she kept rearranging the pieces of nectarine on her cereal.

"You remember Mrs. Martini?" Adriana asked, pressing down on her iron. Although I could not speak Italian, I understood it. Lea spoke it adequately. Mother and Father were both fluent. "Her son was caught stealing again. Seems to run in the family. The grandfather. Well, he wasn't really from here. His mother was from the mainland."

"Oh really, Adriana," Mother said.

"Oh really, Adriana," Lea said, imitating Mother, and I repeated after her, "Oh really, Adriana."

"You shouldn't speak like that to your mother," Adriana said, spitting on the iron then cleaning it with a rag. She continued to iron, her arm moving fast. All her movements were brisk, efficient, even the way she walked around the villa, with short quick steps, and although she was barely five feet tall she gave the impression of being much taller. She had an impressive chest. Her complexion was quite different from most of the islanders, whose skin was rugged and worn from the sunlight. Her skin was unusually white and pink, her hair cut short and black.

I ran my fingers over the rough surface of the dining room table. Like most of the furniture, it was made of rough-hewn stone, carved out of the rock of the island, immovable.

"What about Mr. Peters?" Lea asked.

"Yes, how is he doing?" Mother asked.

"Oh him," Adriana said, shaking her head. "Almost drowned."

"Oh dear, no," Mother said.

"In his bath," Adriana said.

"How can you drown in your bath?" Lea asked.

"Maybe he doesn't know how to swim," I said.

Lea laughed very hard and then I laughed.

"He saw the kidnapping," Adriana said.

"Really?" Mother asked. "Which—"

"Everyone saw it," Adriana said. "Everyone lying on the Cervo beach."

"I wish I had seen it," Lea said. She was staring down at the sole of her foot.

"Me too," I said.

"Here," Adriana said, turning off her iron and walking over to Lea. "Let me see that."

I got up and peered over Lea's shoulder. The black spines of sea urchins were embedded in her foot.

"We must take them out," Adriana said. "They're poisonous."

"Won't they come out on their own in a hot bath?" Mother asked.

After burning the tip of a needle, Adriana sat down on a stool beside Lea and started to extract the spines.

"How did they kidnap him?" Lea asked.

"La cosa più straordinaria è che non . . ."

"They kidnapped the wrong man?" Mother asked.

"Sì," Adriana said.

This seemed extraordinary to me too.

"Did they look alike?" Lea asked just as I was about to ask the same question.

"No," Adriana said.

"Surely," Mother said. She was looking out the window. "Now that they have discovered that he is not the right man, they'll let him go."

"Who knows?" Adriana said, throwing up her hands.

"How dreadful!" Mother said. "But aren't we lucky! The weather seems to have cleared."

The mist had evaporated and the sky was blue and there was just the slightest breeze, not strong enough to stir the curtains or the flowers Adriana had placed in vases. It was already noon. We had slept unusually late. From the dining table, we could see the islands in the distance, sail boats slowly drifting across the sea. Everything seemed so clearly focused, so perfectly defined: the purple bougainvillea, the pink geraniums.

"Do you think they'll cut off his ear?" Lea asked, doing a

handstand against the wall, her nightdress falling down over her head, revealing her pee as we used to call it.

"Really, Lea, what will Adriana think?" Mother said.

"I'm not finished taking out the spines," Adriana said.

Lea jumped back down then sat at the table and started to eat one of the ripe figs from a bowl in the center of the table, and Adriana continued to take out the sea-urchin spines. Mother had left the figs on the windowsill of the kitchen and they had been punctured during the night. Adriana and Lea had laughed when I suggested that mice had eaten them or raccoons. It was more likely to be birds, Adriana said.

"What if they kidnap Dad?" Lea asked. Mother had informed us that he had gone into town. He always liked to buy the *International Herald Tribune.*

"Of course not. Why on earth would they kidnap him?" Mother asked.

"They might think he's a millionaire," Lea said.

"I wouldn't worry about that," Mother said, standing up, leaving her cereal untouched.

I followed Mother into her bedroom. She walked over to the full-length mirror, where she leaned forward and pulled out a white hair from her head. "Do you see any others?" She sat down on the bed and I stood behind her, combing my fingers through her hair. Her hair was soft and light like the sand. Lea had inherited the same, while mine was dark and coarse and thick like Father's. I pulled out another. "You can hardly tell," I said. "Because it's almost the same color."

She drifted over to a desk built into the wall and fingered her notebooks. They were filled with blue ink drawings of the façades of French churches she had traced. She pushed back the cream curtain and stared out at the garden, at the still pine trees, the only movement illusory, the red hibiscus and *amanti del sole* glinting.

"Are you coming?" Lea appeared above the windowsill, waving her floppy white hat before dropping out of sight.

I placed my hand just above Mother's elbow, where her skin was particularly soft. She continued to stand with her gaze fixed on the garden, or perhaps beyond on the pellucid sea. I let go of her arm, crept slowly across the cool red tiles, down the shadowy corridor.

As Lea and I meandered down the same dusty path we had taken the day before, I kept turning thinking I heard Mother's footsteps, catching sight only of a branch shifting back into place, not once of the birds I could hear singing in the dry bushes. Lea stopped by briars of blackberries. I can still see her mouth, her cheek, her hair streaked with blackberry juice. She said that we should pretend it was blood. We had been wounded at war. She wrapped her towel around one arm. I wrapped mine around my waist and dragged my leg. We picked up two sticks and pretended they were sabers. The golfers along the golf course were the distant enemy on their white chariots, their flags flapping in the wind. The white golf balls, cannonballs. Catching sight of two horses trotting behind the Piccolo Pevero beach, we pretended to gallop along the path, hands held in the air. Lea's horse was refractory and shied at every noise. She swerved down the alley leading to Mr. Peters's villa.

With the exception of a small complex of apartments inhabited by local people, the neighborhood surrounding our villa was composed almost exclusively of foreigners. There was the famous piano maker from Germany and his pianist wife; the funeral home director who drove in a hearse to the beach; a best-selling writer of mysteries; the painter Daphne and her husband, Bob; and Mr. Peters, whom Lea and I liked visiting best.

Mr. Peters had once owned a successful construction company in New York City, but after discovering his vocation as a painter, he sold it and bought a small villa on the island. Now and then, to the disgust of the islanders, he did small construction jobs for foreigners. The islanders thought him mad. Twice he had set fire to his villa, having forgotten rags dipped in turpentine.

We loved him for all the reasons the islanders disapproved of him. His untidy villa. The paintings that filled the hallway, the bedroom, the cupboards, even the one bathroom. He did not possess a bed but slept on an old red and white striped couch speckled with paint. We loved the odor of paint and turpentine that pervaded the air, deciphering the scrawls he had written to himself on the walls. I did not understand them but Lea claimed she did. Best of all we loved the way he would let us draw on the walls of his villa.

We stopped to look up at a painting that seemed to have been flung onto the spikes of the gate. The painting was of a woman with red hair. She wore a green dress with gold squares.

The front door to Mr. Peters's villa, painted pink, stood open. The smell of turpentine was even stronger than I remembered. There was just enough room for me to squeeze between canvases stacked on either side of the corridor leading to the living room. A radio Mr. Peters had balanced on top of canvases came tumbling down, but I caught it just before it hit the floor.

The living room was also filled with paintings: paintings hung from the floor to the ceiling. They were propped against walls, against an old wood table, against two chairs with no backs, even along the sides of the red and white striped couch, where Mr. Peters lay asleep.

Lea leaned over the couch, dangling her hair so that the tips touched Mr. Peters's neck. He brushed his neck with his hand. His fingernails were black with paint. His left thumb was missing a nail. His blond hair was uncombed, his face covered by a thin stubble of gold hair. He had a snub nose. He wore his usual khaki pants and shirt spattered with paint. Lea brushed his cheek. He groaned then rubbed his cheek. We laughed. Still he did not wake.

I followed Lea into what had once been the bedroom. Above the outline of the headboard hung more paintings, mostly of women in diaphanous dresses. We could see traces of previous efforts beneath the present paintings. From the portrait of a woman with gold hair who held fish wrapped in a newspaper emerged a woman with dark hair whose eyes seemed to float out of the canvas. From the golf course, which Mr. Peters had painted red, emerged a man dressed in white. Even my untrained eye perceived that none of the paintings were complete. Of our portrait commissioned by our parents three years before, he had drawn only the outline of our figures. He had complained to us on several occasions that it was impossible to paint according to order. He needed his artistic freedom. Our parents explained his eccentricities by saying that he was lonely. The turpentine had gone to his head. But he was entertaining. Sometimes, it was true, he went too far and said inappropriate things. Once he announced to everyone that he hadn't been laid in a year. Lea was quick to explain to me what that meant.

Wandering back into the living room, where Mr. Peters was still sleeping, Lea picked up a paintbrush from a palette and slowly painted over a portrait reminiscent of the Impressionists, a woman with red hair and a green silk dress, almost identical to the painting flung onto the spikes of the gate. Lea drew lines horizontally and then vertically until the whole painting was cut into squares. She had just started to fill in the first box when Mr. Peters sat up, his hair standing on end, his face puffy, his eyes small from sleep.

"What the fuck are you doing?" he said, knocking over several paintings in his haste. Lea dropped the paintbrush but then stood defiantly, one hand on her hip. He stumbled across the room after her but she ran out. I crouched in one corner.

Though I would not have been able to put it into words, I had observed this sort of behavior in Lea before. She would unthinkingly do something very naughty, but if she was called upon, she refused to retract or apologize, and her defiance gave the impression that she had intended to do it all along.

Mr. Peters muttered something under his breath then sat down on the couch. He leaned over, retrieved a half-smoked cigarette from one of the plant holders. He lit the cigarette but put it out.

"You can come out of there," he said.

"Okay," I said, standing.

"When did you arrive?"

"Yesterday."

"You sure got yourself some suntan," he said.

"Yes," I said, touching my nose.

"What do you think of that?" He pointed in the direction of a painting representing four blindfolded men against a white background, divided by a red cross.

"It's different," I said, wanting to please him, though in truth at the time I preferred the paintings of women in diaphanous dresses.

"It's the coat of arms of Bella Terra," he said. "In the seventeenth century, they represented four Moors. They wore headbands to symbolize their royalty, but over the centuries the headbands slipped down and came to symbolize kings transformed into slaves."

"I knew that," Lea said, standing in the doorway. "Did you know that Bella Terra used to be called the Forgotten Island?"

"How come?" I asked.

"Because when America was discovered in 1492, they couldn't be bothered with Bella Terra. They forgot about it completely."

Mr. Peters did not turn to look in her direction.

"I'll let you paint me," she said.

He shrugged then pulled out another cigarette end he had thrown into the plant holder. He lit it and took a puff.

"You always complain you have no models," Lea said.

He hit the heel of one shoe against the floor and flakes of paint came off.

"Go on," she said.

"Oh all right," he said, putting out his cigarette. "I just stretched a canvas this morning."

There was some discussion about where she should pose. Mr. Peters suggested she sit in one of the chairs without backs. I thought she should stand against the plants, but Lea decided she would lie on the couch.

"Whatever, whatever," Mr. Peters said.

Lea threw herself onto the couch. She said she would lie with one arm folded beneath her head, her hair swept to one side. Mr. Peters said he was thinking of something a little more natural, less contrived. Would she not like to turn on her stomach? No, she would not.

I thought Lea most daring. I envied her long blond hair, the delicate bone structure of her face, the blue-green color of her eyes, the way she lay so unself-consciously on the couch, her dress pulled down off one shoulder.

She complained that the light filtering through the window was too bright. It was hurting her eyes. Mr. Peters obliged her by drawing the blind. Her body was now cut horizontally by the shadows of the slats.

"I like it better like that," he said. In the meantime, I found a puzzle made out of pieces of canvas, people's faces and bananas.

From time to time, I looked up to observe Mr. Peters, who was completely absorbed in the composition of his painting. He held his arm before him, squinted with one eye then the other, moved closer then away from the canvas. He hummed some tune I did not recognize.

Lea entertained herself by moving her wrist so that the light caught the face of her wristwatch, projecting a tiny gold circle of light that darted from the wall to the ceiling.

"I need a flower to put behind my ear," Lea said. I agreed reluctantly to get her one. I ran down the corridor, out into the garden, turning back from time to time to glance through the door, but all I could see was a sliver of Mr. Peters's shirt. I broke off the first flower I came to, a pink oleander, then ran back.

"It's bruised," Lea said. "Get me a red one."

"It's fine," I said.

"I want a red one," Lea said.

"Get one yourself then," I said.

"Mr. Peters, she won't get me a flower," Lea said.

"Oh come," Mr. Peters said to me. "Be nice."

I roamed around the garden, hitting overgrown hedges with a branch, stopping to stare at the painting of the woman with red hair flung onto the gate. The gold squares mirrored the sun. I circled the villa several times, waiting for them to call for me, then sat down in the sun on a wood chair that was missing its back. I observed the movements of an iguana until it disappeared between two rocks. The smell of myrtle and rosemary was very strong mixed in with turpentine and the smell of salt. I licked the back of my hand to see if it tasted salty. The sun grew stronger and stronger. I could feel my shoulders—even the top of my head—burning. I had forgotten to put on cream. I would stay until I could bear it no longer. At last I couldn't resist and ran back into the villa.

The tiles felt cool beneath my feet. My eyes took a moment to adjust to the shadowy corridor. Lea lay in the same position I had left her in, but she had slipped off one pink sandal and was dangling the other from her big toe.

"This is getting boring," she said.

"I'm almost done," he said.

"There you are," Lea said, sitting up. "Where's my flower?"

"I forgot," I said.

"Typical." Lea jumped up. She ran over to Mr. Peters and peered at her painting.

"What do you think?" he asked.

"It's okay," she said and shrugged. Before I had a chance to see the painting for myself, she took hold of my hand and pulled me out of the room, pausing only to point to a painting hanging in the corridor of a man. "Who's that?"

"Who do you think it is?" Mr. Peters asked.

"Jimmy Dean," she answered, and he laughed and said, "No, don't you see, it's a portrait of me," and Lea laughed too and said, "No way."

At the villa, we found our parents sitting side by side on the living room couch. Mother was wearing a new cream suit with flat gold buttons that caught the sunlight. Father wore freshly ironed jeans.

"It's our anniversary," Father said. "I bought myself a new pair of shoes. What do you think?" He stretched out his long legs.

"Very nice," Lea said.

"Do you remember the time we bought my engagement ring?"

Mother fingered one of the flat gold buttons. "It was very hot and my fingers swelled in the heat and every ring I tried on was too small and the shop lady said, 'Fancy someone like you having such big fingers?'"

Father laughed and then he said, "What do you think of your mother's new outfit?"

"It's ugly," Lea said.

"That's not very nice," Father said.

Lea blushed.

Mother laughed nervously, letting go of Father's hand to pull Lea's dress, which was still off one shoulder, then touched her hair coiled in back.

"You look so severe like that," Father said. "Why don't you let it down?" Mother shook her head, then smoothed the pleats of her skirt with one hand.

"Oh come on," Father said.

She whispered, "No."

"Don't you think she looks nicer with her hair down?" he asked us.

"Oh yes," we said.

He reached out to touch her hair, but she stood up and said, "Don't."

"Une main de fer dans un gant de velours. A hand of iron in a glove of velvet," he said. I did not understand the expression but laughed loudly, too loudly, and Lea turned and asked me what was so funny and I didn't know what to say. I looked down at the carpet and Father laughed while Mother sat down again and brushed my hair back from my forehead. "You really must be more careful and remember to put sunscreen on," Mother said. "Your forehead is burning. I wouldn't be surprised if you have sunstroke." Her face looked pale and her hand felt cold against my forehead.

3

I recall very little of the next day: the sun through the curtains, highlighting the pattern of pink and yellow flowers looping around blue stripes, wondering whether I should count the flowers that were cut off at the top. Now and then a gust of wind would open the curtains and the scent of myrtle and of juniper would drift into my room. Sometimes Lea would stand between the curtains. Her hair was tangled, her dress covered with the fine ocher dust from the island. I imagined her running down wild paths, jumping over stone walls. Sometimes Adriana would sit beside me and read her Bible, the red cover so worn you could see the green underneath. I liked to trace with one finger the gold letters spelling *Bibbia.* She would recount to me stories from the Bible or about the island. I liked the tales about Bella Terra best. According to all the legends, Bella Terra was a footprint of God's on the sea. Adriana had shown me a map of the island, an old print that hung over the buffet table in the dining area. The shape of the island looked exactly like the outline of a foot. I pictured God stepping from sea to sea. She also told me that the island had once been covered with trees, but that foreign powers had burned the land to track outlaw shepherds, men who had become bandits because of the harsh laws imposed upon them. "Furat chi de su mare venit," she said, narrowing her eyes, using Bella Terra's dialect. I asked her what this meant and she said, "Whoever comes by sea comes to rob us."

"You mean me," I said, pointing to myself.

"No, no, Helenina, you're a baby."

My favorite story of all was about a woman called Lucia Delitala who had a giant mustache and who never got married because she didn't want to depend on a man.

Sometimes Mother would stand in the doorway, one hand resting on the doorknob, her gaze abstracted. I would smell her perfume, so different from the fragrances of the island. As a rule Mother was not very sympathetic to illness. She was fond of saying, "I've never been sick for more than a day," her only weakness an arrhythmia that forced her to slow down. I remember her spreading cool calamine on my skin.

Often, I would pretend to sleep. I would picture the sun on the water, the seagulls, the islands in the distance. Once, Lea asked if I could go visiting, but Mother said that I needed to stay out of the sun. I could go the next day.

When the next day came, however, Lea went to the painter's villa without me. She said she would not speak to me again if I followed her and so I watched from beneath the archway leading to the villa, until she had disappeared from sight.

I spent my time with Mother. She had always enjoyed baths but that summer she took three, sometimes four, baths a day. Even as a child I knew that it wasn't only because of the heat. I liked to sit in the bathroom with her, watching the way the light flickered through the bougainvillea onto the blue-gray diamond tiles, listening to her stories. My favorite were the ones about her friend Prue, who had traveled through Europe with her. I liked hearing about how Prue had persuaded Mother to sleep on top of bathing houses in Italy, to slip into hotels and take baths in empty suites. Or the time Prue had persuaded Italian boys to order pizzas for them then skipped out the back door. I could not imagine Mother doing these things. She said herself that she used to be different. I could not reconcile the person she was then with the person she was now—sad, studious, restrained. She was always studying. She rarely laughed and sometimes I would hear her crying from behind a closed door.

The third afternoon after our visit to Mr. Peters's villa, Mother closed the heavy wood shutters in her room. When I asked where Father had gone, she said that he was discussing plans with the architect.

"Plans to do what?" I asked.

"Plans to build a swimming pool."

"But you don't want a swimming pool."

"What does it matter what I want?"

I opened and closed the cream curtains because I liked the sound of the curtain rings gliding along the rod, until Mother asked me to stop. "Why don't you play with Lea?" she asked. I continued to stand by the window, hesitating whether to venture out or to lie beside Mother, who already had slipped between the cool fragrant white sheets. I liked to curl up beside her, but she said again, "Go on, darling."

After the dark room, the sun seemed particularly bright. I

wished I owned grown-up glasses like Lea's. Mine were for babies, the light blue glass ineffective; worse still the rims were pink and heart shaped. The sun was so strong that the tarred driveways felt wobbly beneath my feet, like stepping on jellyfish.

There was no sign of Lea down the usual dirt path. I wondered if perhaps she had taken a different route, one that involved traversing through private property past dogs. I was terrified of the dogs. They were boxers and they drooled, their saliva hanging in long streams that glistened in the sun. Coming around one corner, however, I caught sight of her, throwing her white hat up in the air and catching it. She ran over to a bush and picked blackberries, cramming them into her mouth, peered over a hedge. She stopped by a mailbox and slipped a piece of paper inside. I waited for her to turn the next corner, before opening the mailbox and reading her note. She had scribbled, "Dear Mr. Roberto, You have not payed attention to my advice. Your end is near. Sincerely, L.D."

I shadowed her all the way to Mr. Peters's villa. Lea was peering through the crack of one shutter. The villa looked closed. The rest of the shutters were shut. The pink door locked. Lea did not say anything when I ran over to her. She seemed to have known all along that I had been following her.

She told me to get her a stick, which she inserted between the shutters that led to the bathroom. The shutters opened and she crawled into the house and I went after her.

The villa was filled with shadows. In the dim light I could make out only the top layer of the paintings. The lady with dark hair and the man dressed in white had disappeared. Mr. Peters did not lie on his couch. Something brushed against me and I cried out, but it was just one of his ferns. I was glad when Lea threw open a shutter and sunlight flooded the room, illuminating the portrait of the woman with red hair that Lea had started to paint over on our first visit, only now instead of a green dress the woman was clothed in pink.

I might not have noticed Lea's painting, standing in one corner, if Lea had not marched over and pulled off the drop cloth covering it.

"You're naked," I exclaimed. But Lea did not respond, just jabbed the canvas with one finger. I could not believe that she had posed naked. Even my inexperienced eye could see that this painting was different. Whereas often the faces of the women Mr. Peters painted seemed out of magazines, he had succeeded in capturing Lea's expression, the look that challenged rather than submitted; even the colors seemed more true to life, the blue-green of Lea's eyes, the red of the couch. He had painted the tiny gold watch.

"Look," I said, turning to Lea. "He painted the flower yellow instead of red and the couch has no stripes."

Lea handed me a can of something. I took it from her then looked at it—the label had come off but I could tell by the strong odor that it was turpentine.

"What—"

"We're going to burn it," she said.

"What?"

"The painting," she said.

I presumed she wanted to burn it because she was now ashamed at having allowed Mr. Peters to paint her naked.

"You have to burn it," she said.

"Why?"

"Because he's bound to suspect me. He'll check for my fingerprints."

I sensed that what we were doing was not the same as the detective games we often played together.

"Go on," she said. "Splatter it."

I was nervous about getting the turpentine on something other than the painting. I lifted the can carefully, as close to the canvas as possible, dribbling a few drops, but Lea grabbed it from me and doused the canvas. I was afraid that she had got some on her dress. She pulled a box of matches from her pocket, then lit a match and threw it against the canvas. It caught fire immediately. We watched the canvas burn, melt, Lea's figure gradually curl and disappear. I would probably have just stood and watched the whole canvas be consumed if Lea had not taken me by the hand. We ran through the corridor, knocking over paintings and books on our way. The radio crashed to the floor then turned on. Voices echoed after us. We scrambled up the hill, through dry bushes, past the hibiscuses. I laughed and laughed hysterically but Lea stood with her arms crossed, looking down at me, her expression serious, until at last I too became silent.

As we were about to enter the archway that led to the villa, we caught sight of Mother backing the Jeep out of the driveway. This was most extraordinary. The Jeep was extremely hard to put in gear, even steering required a great effort, and it was parked on a sharp incline. Mother always insisted on Father driving it out of the parking spot.

My first thought was that Mother had seen smoke coming from the painter's villa. Perhaps she had even caught sight of Lea and me running out of his house. She had figured out what we had done. I expected her to stop beside us, but she drove right by the bushes we were hiding behind, a cloud of dust rising on either side of the Jeep.

It was only after she had disappeared and the dust had settled that I noticed Father standing beneath a pine tree. Lea ran over to him. She said something I could not hear, then they turned and drifted down the path, arm under arm. I knew that Lea was angry with Mother but I didn't understand why.

For a long time, I stood staring over the hibiscuses at the dust rising from the road, expecting Mother to return.

4

The next morning Lea shook me awake. She said that Mr. Peters had just peered into the window of our bedroom. "Is Mum back?" I asked, and she said, "Yes, yes, she came back a few hours ago. Come on. Hurry." We ran out into the garden. The tiles were still cool. We could hear the *pshiut, pshiut* of the sprinklers. The gardenias and the *amanti del sole* glimmered. We caught sight of Adriana's husband, a frail man with luminous brown eyes. There was no sign of Mr. Peters.

I kept expecting Mr. Peters to arrive. Lea's games did not succeed in distracting me. Assassin was our favorite game that summer. In order to play we needed a victim, a witness, a detective, and of course an assassin. We could dispense with the witness but not with a victim. Most often we called upon Adriana's niece, Carla. Lea pulled out an imaginary knife from her pocket as she sat astride Carla and pretended to stab her as I watched from behind the door.

"Ugh, ugh," Carla screamed. Lea kept stabbing her. Carla asked if she could stop screaming. "Am I not dead?" she asked.

Lea said, "No, keep screaming."

I stepped from behind the door and whipped out an imaginary notepad and wrote down details about the crime.

After that, Lea and I lay on our beds until Lea suggested we pretend to be Mother and Father. I played Mother and Lea played Father. She threw a book across the room. I burst into tears then rushed into the bathroom. We fell upon the bed and groaned and cried. Suddenly I caught sight of Mother reflected in the mirror. I heard the sound of her sandals as she ran down the corridor.

I raced after her, but when I arrived at her bedroom door it was closed. Mother and Father were talking, arguing perhaps. I could not hear well enough to make it out.

When Lea and I returned a little later, our parents were no longer in their room. Lea dived onto their bed, noticed a magazine of nude ladies sticking out from between the mattress and the boxspring. I had never seen pictures of naked ladies before. One woman had her legs wide open. "Disgusting," we roared. Lea suggested that we cut the pictures out and make a collage of them. We laughed and laughed as she cut a heart out of a piece of red paper then pasted nude pictures on the outside. Inside the card we wrote, "Happy Anniversary, Mum and Dad."

I crept after Lea into the living room. Lea presented them the card. Mother said, "Really," and Father, "What on earth!" They would not open the card. "You're to go to your room immediately," Father said.

When Mr. Peters did appear, we were sitting on Lea's bed, staring out the window of our bedroom. I could have reached out and touched his dirty blond hair. Lea even called out *coucou* but he did not look up. He was quite deaf from the construction work he used to do.

We shadowed him as he circled round the house, peering into the windows. From behind a bush we watched Mother open the door to the living room to let him in. He sat down on a stool opposite her. He leaned forward, then pulled the waist of his trousers over his belt. He did not wear his belt through the loops of his pants but like an elastic band. Through the holes in his shoes I could see bright orange socks. I expected him to tell her what we had done, but he did not, and Mother went into the kitchen.

We crept up closer to the glass window, giggling when we caught sight of Mr. Peters pulling gum from his mouth and then sticking it beneath the coffee table.

When Mother returned with Mr. Peters's drink, I thought he would tell her what we had done. But they sat without talking, their glasses balanced on their knees. Mr. Peters swallowed his drink down in one gulp then placed his glass on the table. He leaned forward and played with the tongue of one of his shoes. He kept clenching his jaw, making the muscles of his neck stand out.

It was only when Father appeared that they started to talk. Father asked how our portrait was coming. Mr. Peters said that he had just a few finishing touches. The color of our dresses was not quite the right shade of blue. I could not believe he was lying, and in my mind I pictured the painting he described: the straw hats he said we wore, the identical dresses with pink sashes. Then he went on to bemoan his lack of success. No one recognized his genius. What could he do?

Mother said she was sure that eventually the great public would not fail to be convinced. Father asked if he was submitting slides. Mr. Peters said he had no money. Father then told one of his favorite jokes about the man who kept complaining to God that he was not winning the lottery. Finally, God appeared and said, "First, you have to buy a ticket." Mother gave examples of painters who were recognized late in life. What about Gauguin? she said. Van Gogh was recognized posthumously.

"Great," he said, and they laughed.

They talked politics, mostly American politics since Mr. Peters was American. Father said he had never trusted Nixon, while Mother admitted that he had fooled her completely. Mr. Peters's voice took on a vociferous tone, he went bright red, and kept repeating "the fucking bastard."

At last, he looked down at his hands, scratched his head. I thought again he seemed about to say something. But he just glanced at Mother, who kept folding her red paper napkin. He said he had work to do and reached discreetly for his chewing gum under the table. "Putrid," Lea said, and I repeated, "Putrid."

We followed him down the asphalt road, onto the dirt path that led to his villa. I was surprised to see the villa still standing. In my mind, it had gone up in flames along with the painting. With a kick he opened the pink front door and disappeared inside.

5

The next morning Mother was gone. This time she had taken her suitcase and packed our favorite dress of hers, the color of daffodils. The wind started to blow; the cool mistral from the north. There were terrible fires on the other side of the island. A boy and his mother burned, trapped in their car.

I kept drifting in and out of the villa, lingering by the telephone, watching Adriana iron, pestering her to tell me more stories. She told me about her extended family, how they all lived in the same apartment building. She lived with her husband and her mother on the first floor, across from her brother and his wife and two boys. Her mother-in-law lived in an apartment below theirs, and several cousins inhabited the second floor. I loved the idea of a whole family living in the same building. Our grand-fathers had died before we were born and our grandmothers lived far away, one in America, the other in South Africa. We had no family in Paris.

"Everyone is related on the island," she said. I begged her to tell me more stories about bandits. She described to me again the way they would hide in the *macchia* and wait for the rich to come through, then stop their carriages and force them to hand over their jewels or lose their lives. I wanted Lea to play bandit, but she said she was not in the mood. I would not help her sweep the bougainvillea and, for the first time, I refused to get her sunglasses. I stood and watched the wind blow the bougainvillea from one side to the other of the veranda. At first the flowers were bright purple, but gradually they lost their color, becoming transparent vessels.

When Mother did call, I was out in the garden and Lea got to the telephone first. I squeezed as close to her as I could. She smelled of oranges. I kept trying to pull the receiver from Lea. Then Mother must have asked her to put me on. She asked me how I was and I whispered fine, feeling self-conscious, because Lea and Father were watching me. She said that she loved me and that she would come and visit us soon but that she needed a few days to herself. I replaced the receiver carefully.

Later I followed Lea and Father as they meandered through the garden. Father said he did not feel like going to the beach. He did not feel like playing cards. He assured us Mother would be back soon.

They swung in the hammock. Father, catching sight of me, called out, "Helen," and raised one arm, but I ran to the end of the garden and climbed the wall. Now and then a car drove by in a cloud of dust. In the distance buildings quivered as if underwater.

Walking back toward the hammock where Father and Lea still were, I sang loudly a French song about angels coming from the mountain. I had been told at school that I had a sweet voice and so I imagined that I could impress Father by singing. Father and Lea started to sing gloria, imitating my intonation, then they laughed.

At dinner that night, Father remarked how pretty I looked. I tried very hard not to blush. I thought that I was blushing for him, for saying what I knew was not true. "How nicely you did your hair," he said, glancing at Lea. Her hair was tangled in a knot down her back. She kicked me under the table and I said, "Ow," and Father said, "Now that's not very nice, Lea," and smiled.

Father imitated the way Lea slurped her soup. She laughed and said, "You've dropped soup on your shirt." Turning to me, but still addressing Lea, he said, "And look how Helen uses her fingers to push her bread into her mouth. The fork is not enough." Tears came to my eyes and I started to get up.

"Oh, come on," he said. "Don't be such a baby." He turned to Lea. "And who taught you to hold your fork like that? You look as if you're going to stab someone."

Lea laughed again and said, "You chew with your mouth open."

"Don't you talk to me like that," he said. "You're to treat me with respect."

Lea grew quiet but pulled the skirt of my dress under the table. I continued to eat carefully, trying not to use my fingers.

Just then we heard a car stop outside our villa. Lea and I ran outside. I hoped it was Mother, but instead a police car stood outside the archway. I thought of the painting Lea and I had burned. We would soon be arrested. Lea and I ducked behind a bush then circled back around the villa and peered into the living room. A man stood with his back to the glass door. We could not hear what he said. Father had closed the door. The man turned slightly toward us, as if he sensed our presence, and reached for something in his pocket. I'm sure he saw Lea and me crouching by the door, but he did not acknowledge our presence. He simply squeezed out cream from a bottle and slowly massaged it into his hands. To this day I do not know the nature of his visit, whether it was to talk to Father about the fire and his suspicions. More likely, it had to do with one of the numerous regulations. Perhaps he was there to tell Father that the pine trees in front of the parking lot had grown taller than the regulated height. They blocked the view of the ocean from one of the villas. But at the time I did not think that the police would be sent just for that. I felt sure they had come to investigate the matter of the burned painting.

6

The afternoon of the Ashtons' arrival the green flag was still up at the beach. We could go swimming. But striped umbrellas were tethered with rocks and shoes. Now and then, one of the umbrellas would escape and a shout would go up and everyone would exclaim how dangerous these umbrellas were, how someone might get impaled.

I lay behind the dunes, where there were no people and the sand was fine and soft. I played a game of placing my hand flat on one of the yellow nettles, slowly lowering my hand until I felt my palm prick. I watched Lea doing handstands along the shore. Lea could balance herself for a very long time with her legs straight up in the air. In the distance I saw a motorboat pulling a water-skier. The man driving the boat kept turning and gesturing with one arm, yelling at the same time something to the water-skier. The water was so choppy I was surprised anyone would want to ski.

A Jeep chugged down the path strictly forbidden to cars, a cloud of dust rising in its wake. Someone waved, shouted "Yoo-hoo." People turned to stare.

Though it would have been most uncharacteristic of her, I

imagined that it was Mother. But then I remembered that Father had mentioned that the Ashtons were supposed to arrive that morning. Every year, they intended to visit, but always, at the very last minute, something would prevent them. The year before, one of their dogs had gotten ill.

But this year, when the call came, Father had been insistent. I heard him say several times, "You must come," and then later, "As her oldest friend. Don't you understand? She won't talk to me."

Mrs. Ashton was a striking woman, tall, close to six feet, her long brown hair flecked with red, her skin a creamy olive. Though she was Mother's oldest friend and Lea's godmother, I had met her only once on a brief visit to London. Mother and I had spent the afternoon with her, while Father and Lea had gone to Wimbledon. Lea had never made her acquaintance. Until that summer, Mrs. Ashton had showed no interest in her. Not once had she sent a card or a gift. Her only contribution was Lea's name. Mrs. Ashton had suggested Ileana. Her family was originally from Greece, and I had heard Mother say that she looked as if she had stepped out from a Greek urn. On that first morning she wore a green silk robe.

She strode across the sand beside Father, head held high, shoulders back.

Lea curtsied in the formal manner she had been taught in France. "How do you do?" she said, putting out her hand. But Mrs. Ashton did not seem to notice her. She untied her robe, letting it drop onto the sand.

"Say hello to Prue," Father reminded me.

I dusted the sand off my hands before holding out my right hand. But instead of shaking it, Prue placed her towel over my arm, then ran toward the water. I later found out—Prue told Lea who told me—that the towel's initials, though they corresponded to Prue's, P.A., actually stood for the name of some hotel. The Ashtons owned a suitcase that was filled with articles from hotels: sample shampoos, creams, soaps, perfumes, miniature bottles of liquor, even sheets and robes.

Mrs. Ashton swam the crawl, arms slicing the water. She swam far beyond the dark waters Lea and I had ventured into. I had once heard Mother say that Prue was a bit mad. She had modeled for painters as a young girl and was now an artist herself. From our one visit, I remembered seeing in her studio dresses encased in glass, a wedding gown of white lace that had belonged to Prue's great-grandmother preserved in beeswax, and in particular pencil drawings of a girl who had set herself on fire. The drawings of the girl appeared everywhere, in between bookshelves, even in the bathroom, inside a closet, lit by an electric light. The drawings were crude and frightening, almost identical, the flame obscuring the figure completely, only the feet of the girl appearing from beneath the flame. I remembered asking Mother who the girl was and Mother saying that she thought it was someone Prue had met at the hospital.

Father, Lea, and I sat side by side on Prue's towel.

"How long are the Ashtons staying?" Lea asked Father.

"I don't know," Father said. "A week or two, I guess."

"What's Mr. Ashton like?" Lea said. "How come he didn't come to the beach?"

"I don't know," Father said. "I think Prue told him to unpack. You'll soon meet him." He threw a handful of sand at Lea's legs. Lea threw a handful of sand at him.

The wind blew and the sand brushed against a woman sitting under the umbrella next to ours.

"Attenzione," the woman said in a plaintive voice.

"Attenzione," Father said imitating her voice, in sotto voce.

"Attenzione," Lea said, and Father laughed.

When Prue stepped out of the water, she continued to ignore Lea and me. She dried herself carefully then strode across the beach, Father following a few steps behind. She laughed when Father discovered a fine on the dashboard of his Jeep, saying "Oh well!" She did not offer to pay for it, and Lea later told me that Father had told her that though the Ashtons appeared rich and seemed to spend their time traveling the world, they had, in fact, very little money and were living beyond their means.

In the Jeep, with the windows wide open, I could not hear all that was being said in front. Lea had squeezed between the front two seats, blocking my view. I heard Prue say, "Don't look so glum," and caught sight in the rearview mirror of Father smiling.

When the car stopped in front of the villa, Prue continued to sit in the front seat of the Jeep, even after Father had gone round and opened the door. She seemed completely absorbed in her own thoughts and unaware of her surroundings. I wondered if she was trying to devise the best strategy to get Mother to return.

On the path to the villa, there was not enough room for the

four of us abreast. Prue walked between Father and Lea. On the back of her green robe a gold dragon with a blue tongue flashed.

Adriana sat making fresh pasta at the kitchen table. She did not say hello. Probably she was annoyed by the extra work involved in the Ashtons' visit. I followed Lea, who followed Prue down the corridor, but when we reached her room, Lea turned and whispered, "Do you have to follow me everywhere?"

Just before Lea closed the door, I caught a glimpse of the Ashtons' room. Two leather suitcases lay across the bed. Binoculars hung over the back of one of the chairs. The crimson curtains were drawn and everything glowed pink. Mr. Ashton's face was reflected in the mirror. He was standing, smoothing both sides of his hair with the flat of his hands.

I ran back to the kitchen and helped Adriana cut the green dough into long thin strips to make tagliatelle verde. Mother always said that Adriana was an extraordinary cook but very secretive about her recipes. If Mother asked for the ingredients, Adriana would say a little of this, a little of that, but never the exact quantities. I kept nibbling on *carta musica*, a specialty of the island, crispy bread so thin it was like parchment. Adriana always heated it up and added a drop of olive oil before serving it to me.

When Lea emerged from the Ashtons' room, she declared Prue's silk green robe divine. She told me that Prue had traveled around the world. She had shown Lea a photograph of three white dogs she owned who looked like pigs. One of the dogs had drowned in her pool. Lea imitated the way Prue sashayed across the room, the way she said "dear." "How would you like to pass me that towel, dear?" I wanted to take turns, but she would not let

51

me. As for Mr. Ashton, Lea had found him disappointing. He was much older than Prue; forty, she said. He was overweight. He and Prue were the same height but he looked much shorter. He talked about birds and liked to hunt. Father said he was to the right of Genghis Khan. We did not know what that meant but the way he raised his eyebrow and his tone of voice indicated that it was not something to be desired. Mr. Ashton made jokes even Lea did not understand. He smoked cigars.

Lea wanted to know all about Prue, but that afternoon the Ashtons and Father spent their time on the veranda beneath the pergola, shadows cast on their faces and arms by the wisteria above them like strange tattoos of snakes and flowers. From time to time, Father and Mrs. Ashton leaned forward: heads close together, they whispered, while Mr. Ashton sat across from them, twirling the ice cubes in his drink with one of the swizzle sticks we liked to steal because of the little animals at the top of each stick. Now and again, Mrs. Ashton would lean forward and pass Mr. Ashton her glass and he would trot into the villa, returning a few minutes later with her glass full. Once Lea crept up and Father turned and said, "I thought I told you to go play."

"I don't want to play," Lea said, implying that she was too old. She skipped down the path leading away from Mr. Peters's house and the beach, past the property of eccentric English who kept sheep instead of a lawn mower. The sheep bleated to one another at different pitches, some low, some high. Lea could imitate them to perfection and they responded to her, making me laugh. The wind blew and dust rose from the path. The scent of myrtle and pine pervaded the air. In the distance, the roofs of hotels glinted. I wondered in which hotel Mother was staying. She had never done this before. Father was the one who was frequently absent. She hated being apart from us for even a day. She liked to tell us the story of the first time she came on her own with Father to Bella Terra. She was so homesick for us that she returned to Paris after three days.

Lea and I practiced our special walk, marching for two steps then skipping so that our feet came down at the same time.

I can still picture our two silhouettes, the big floppy hat I wore with the strings left untied. Every now and then I would have to readjust the hat when a piece of straw stuck through a hole and tickled my scalp.

When we returned, it was much later, but the grown-ups were still on the veranda. Mr. Ashton pointed to a bird that fluttered by the gardenias. Lea looked through the binoculars first. Mr. Ashton said that it was a very rare bird. It was no bigger than a gardenia flower and fluttered in midair.

Then Lea said, "I see Mum."

"It's my turn," I pulled on her arm.

"Wait," she said.

"Come on." I pulled on her arm again.

She continued to stare. "She's wearing a pale green dress."

"Give it to me," I said.

"She's talking to Mr. Peters," she said.

"Who's Mr. Peters?" Prue asked.

"A painter," Father said.

"Is she coming home?" I asked.

"I don't know," Lea said. "She's still talking to him."

At last, I could not stand it. I grabbed the binoculars from Lea's hands. We rolled across the floor. "Be careful," Mr. Ashton said. Father told me to stop. He tried to pull me away from Lea. "Stop," Mr. Ashton said again.

All of a sudden the binoculars flew out of our hands, landing with a crash against the wall. I heard one of the lenses crack.

Mr. Ashton picked up the binoculars, tilted them. A tiny piece of glass flew out. He stared at me with mournful eyes. They were the palest blue color.

"You're both to go to your room immediately," Father said.

I followed Lea across the patio down steps into our room. She sat cross-legged on her bed with her back to me. She pulled out a box of old cards. I stared at her back where the straps of her overalls had shifted, showing the white lines where her skin had not been touched by the sun.

Later I heard Mr. Peters say, "Four of hearts." His voice floated up from the living room. Because he was hard of hearing, he would sometimes shout without realizing it. This was particularly true when he was on the phone, or when he got excited.

Lea no longer sat on her bed. Leaning out the casement window, I saw that she was standing on the veranda behind the partially closed blind. The wind had died but every now and then a gust would blow through the living room and the candles would flicker. I could just discern the tip of Mr. Ashton's cigar. The electricity had gone out but it was not yet dark; the sky cast an orange shadow across the sea. It caught Mrs. Ashton's long, almost red hair. "Do pay attention, darling," I heard her say to Mr. Ashton.

I stepped onto the veranda and stood right beside Lea. The wind blew and I felt her hair brush my face. Bougainvillea drifted across the tiled floor. The sound of grown-up voices floated out, the scent of the cigar too strong and sweet. But Lea did not turn.

A candle stood on the kitchen table before Adriana, illuminating her face, sad in repose, the features relaxing, the eyes seeming to droop, the lips, even the cheeks. But as soon as she spoke the impression disappeared. I attributed her sadness to her multiple miscarriages, picturing dozens of small coffins floating out to sea. Only a month before our arrival she had lost a child. I had heard her tell Mother that she had had to give the clothes she had knitted all winter to her sister who was also expecting. Even as a child I sensed that the album in which she kept newspaper clippings of all the disasters that had occurred on the island, from the fires to the kidnappings, was somehow connected with her secret unhappiness. I leaned against the table, seeing upside down the yellowing newspaper clippings affixed to black pages. She told us that Bella Terra had been subjected to more woes than any island, not only invaders but also plagues.

She pointed to a photograph of a man standing between his wife and child. He was smiling and wore a mustache. "Poor man," she said. "They found him."

"Who?" I asked.

"The man they kidnapped by mistake," she said.

"Where?"

"Two bullets. One here and one there." She poked my shoulder and my chest to show me where the bullets had gone in.

"But he's with his wife and daughter," I said, pointing to the photograph.

"That was before," she sighed.

Adriana flipped to the beginning of the album, stopping at a picture that was so faded I could make out only the outline. "Now this woman had a tragic life," she said. She told us that the woman was betrothed to a man, but shortly before her betrothal she fell in love with another man. She went to see her priest, who told her she must not break her promise. The first night after her wedding she dreamed that her husband was going to kill her. Three months later he chased her with a kitchen knife. He was locked up in an asylum, but every Sunday she would visit him.

"Why didn't she marry the man she loved before?" I asked.

"It was too late," she said.

"You should never listen to priests," Lea said.

"Not at all," Adriana said.

"What else happened to her?" I asked.

"She woke up one morning completely blind," Adriana said.

"You made that up," Lea said.

"I did not," she said.

"You did," Lea said.

"Now run along and play," Adriana said.

"Tell us about your cousin," Lea asked.

"Which cousin?" Adriana asked.

"The one in jail," she said.

"I don't know what you are talking about," Adriana said.

I begged Lea to tell me about Adriana's cousin but she would not. She suggested we play blind man. She said I had to be the blind man because it was her idea. I let her blindfold me and lead me down the corridor. I heard her open a door. She led me into a room, pushed me onto an unmade bed. I pulled off my blindfold. She had led me to the Ashtons' room.

I did not dare touch anything. I watched Lea leaf through books. Most of them were on birds. Noticing a collection of pillboxes on top of a chest of drawers, she slipped one in the shape of an egg into her pocket. I noticed a green box in the shape of a hexagon, carved out of jade. Inside it was another box and inside that another. The smallest one was the tiniest box I had ever seen. I placed them in a row then put them back together. Lea opened the drawers to the chest, touched Mrs. Ashton's silk underwear. She found inside a briefcase, dozens of unopened packs of cards. I thought I heard someone in the corridor but it was just the grown-up voices drifting from the veranda. Lea said we could go, and so we wandered out into the garden over to the hammock, strung between two pines, a gold net in the reflection of the last rays of sun. We stared up at the swallows darting through the sky. They flew high, shuddering then sailing on, carried by the wind.

7

The morning following the Ashtons' arrival, the red flag was up. There were only two or three people on the beach. The dock had detached itself from its moors and drifted out to sea. Umbrellas floated upside down, even beach chairs had been swept out. The sea had submerged the sandy dunes where Lea and I had played only a few days before.

Perched on a rock, I stared at the water where the sea had churned up the sand. Masses of seaweed had floated to shore. I did not like to swim through seaweed; the way it stuck to my arms and legs made me think of eels. Lea drifted far out, ignoring the whistles of the coast guard. Now and then she disappeared completely from sight.

Her first words when she reached the shore regarded Mrs. Ashton, or "Prue" as she now called her. Do you think she'll be up when we get back? Do you think she'll want to go swimming? She requested that I tell her everything I remembered from my visit with Mother to Prue's house, but before I could describe it she asked question after question as we walked up the hill to the villa. "She was sent to an asylum at sixteen, right?" she asked. "I don't know," I said, but seeing that this kind of answer was not what she wanted I switched to saying yes, no matter how preposterous the suggestion. I agreed that Mrs. Ashton had thrown herself onto train tracks. She had dozens of boyfriends at a time. She had got her period at eight years old. Lea herself had got her period only a few months before and was very proud of the sanitary napkins she now used. She enjoyed going up to the counter at the pharmacy and asking for them in a loud voice. I could not imagine doing such a thing; just thinking about it made me blush. "Can you imagine getting your period at eight?" Lea continued. "Mum said that Prue didn't know what it was. She thought she was going to die." According to Lea, Mother had told another friend that Prue had made a sculpture of her first boyfriend's penis. She had made it into a fountain. Mother had giggled as she demonstrated the length with her hands, scary, she had said, stopping to talk as soon as she caught sight of Lea.

I was pleased to remember one detail I knew Lea would like. Before owning three dogs, I told Lea, Prue owned a monkey. She adored the monkey until it grew old and one day turned on her and bit her.

At the villa, Lea and I listened at Prue's door. Lea dared me to knock, which I did but so timorously that no one came. Lea knocked loudly and we heard Prue say, "Come in." Through the open door we could see her long legs, a fold of her white robe. "Come in," she repeated, and Lea pushed open the door. Prue was leaning forward into the mirror, adjusting an earring in one nostril. I had never known anyone to do this before and stared with great interest. She told me that she had done it in India. Lea asked if she could spray perfume from a small bottle with a pink nozzle, filling the room with a scent that made me sneeze.

"Now do you girls have any messages to relay to your Mother?" Prue asked.

I looked down at my hands. I kept bending the fingers of one hand back. I could not think of anything.

I did not look up when Prue asked, "Shall I say that you love her very much and that you want her to come back?"

"Yes," I whispered.

We followed her down the corridor.

Instead of proceeding immediately to the Jeep, however, Prue insisted on having eggs and bacon. "A light breakfast, really," she said. "No lamb chops or kippers."

"But it's almost lunchtime," Adriana said, and Prue responded, waving one hand in the air, "Oh don't worry, I won't have any lunch," as if this resolved the issue. She told us about her family. How her mother was a dentist's assistant and her father a dentist. "Imagine," she said, "they met over teeth." She told us about an aunt who refused to leave her bedroom, her food brought on a tray by her brother. I wanted to hear about the asylum but did not dare bring it up. Her first real boyfriend had committed suicide when she was sixteen. I imagined that it was because he was madly in love with her and that she had rejected him.

"What about the girl on fire?" I asked.

"Ah, so you remember that," she said. Lea looked at me askance. She seemed to think my omission deliberate. But I had forgotten to relay to her that particular detail.

"She set herself on fire," Prue said.

I tried to picture how someone could do such a thing, but I couldn't.

"How?" I asked.

"She wrapped herself in a towel and set fire to it," she said.

At this point, Mr. Ashton and Father appeared. "I saw a Marmora's Warbler," Mr. Ashton said.

"I've never understood what he sees in birds. Do you?" Prue addressed us. "Tigers, snakes, yes, but birds?" We laughed. "When I first met Mr. Ashton he was not interested in birds. He pretended to be interested in foreign movies. But the truth is that he hates them. He can't be bothered with the subtitles! You fooled me, dear." Mrs. Ashton always talked in this mocking way to her husband. Lea liked to imitate her blasé tone.

Then Prue said it was time for her to call Mother. Everyone watched as she picked up the receiver and pressed the red button. She shook her head. "There's no dial tone," she said. The phone was out of order. This happened so frequently that we simply waited for it to work again. There was no point in going to a neighbor to call from their phone because it would take forever to get through to the telephone company.

Prue suggested we play bridge while we waited. They needed a fourth and Lea volunteered. I did not enjoy playing bridge. Even when Mother was my partner, my hands would tremble and I would lose track of the cards. I would forget how many trumps had been played.

At the table, I drew pictures of tiny people against giant hills. I kept glancing up, admiring the way Lea sat playing with the grown-ups, one leg over the side of the chair, from time to time

swinging her long hair out of her face. She played with con-
centration. At first she and Father won. "Good for you," Father
said to Lea. "Chip off the old block." But then they were unlucky.
The Ashtons had extraordinary cards, and despite Father and
Lea's best efforts they started to lose. Father told Lea that she
might concentrate better if she didn't have her hair flopping in
her eyes. Why did she not sit properly? The rug was curled up
beneath her chair.

"Sometimes there's nothing to be done when you run out of
luck," Prue said.

"But she's flashing her cards in your faces," Father said.

"Chest your cards," Mr. Ashton said, putting out his cigar.

"From what I can see there's not much to hide," Prue said.

"Shit," Father said to Lea, "what's the point of playing?" He
threw his cards down on the table.

"Come on," Prue said, "I was just joking."

They played all morning, stopping only for lunch, which Prue
enjoyed despite her earlier assertions, resuming immediately
after. Father was determined to make up his loss. But they
continued to lose steadily. "Shit," Father said to Lea, "why
did you play that? Didn't you notice that the ace of clubs had
been played?"

Prue suggested they change partners, girls against boys. Father
said it was a bit late for that.

I lay on the tiled floor listening to the sound of the sand
blowing against the glass, stared at the sea covered with white-
caps.

It was only around four that Prue reached Mother. Mother had been to see a real El Greco in the church of Stella Maris in Porto Santa, Prue said. Adriana related to me later that the painting was a gift by a German industrial family in gratitude for the recovery of a relative. I looked to Father to see if he was pleased, but he seemed absorbed by his defeat. He and Lea had been soundly beaten, and they were silent as we followed the Ashtons up to the parking lot. The stones were so hot that I ran. I could not understand how Lea, who was also barefoot, could stand to walk. As we watched the Ashtons get into the Jeep, Father placed his hand on my shoulder. I remember the weight of his hand, wondering how I should hold myself, whether to stand absolutely still, or on the contrary to move and to somehow acknowledge his hand.

When Lea ran down the hill, I followed her. She screamed "fried" whenever she passed through the sunlight. She zigzagged across the green golf course, her arms outstretched. Then she lay on her back, ignoring my collection of soggy white golf balls covered in grass and mud.

Because of the wind, the golf course was deserted. We had it all to ourselves.

But Lea refused to play and so I continued to look for balls, waiting for the Ashtons to return.

When at last I heard the Jeep, I interpreted the speed of its approach as a sign that Prue had been successful. They could not wait to get back to the villa. Even when I caught sight of the Jeep with no one in the backseat, Prue behind the wheel and Mr. Ashton beside her, I imagined that Mother was somehow concealed. It was only after peering through each window that I had to acknowledge that I was mistaken. Even then I had to ask, "Where's Mum?" as if the Ashtons had hidden her somewhere.

Placing one hand on Lea's shoulder, the other on mine, Prue said that it was too much to expect that she should succeed in persuading Mother to return to the villa after just one visit. She told us not to despair. She was sure that, with time, she would manage to change Mother's mind.

I wished they would let me try. I felt certain that I could persuade her.

"It's always important to look on the bright side of things. Isn't that right, dear?" She turned to glance back at Mr. Ashton, who looked down and mumbled something incomprehensible before taking a path that led to the bottom of the garden, while we proceeded to the villa.

Father stood at the entrance. Prue took him by the elbow, and he motioned for us to go to our room, but from our bedroom window we could hear them.

"Six years. I had no idea," Prue said.

"Yes, six years," Father said matter of factly, as if he couldn't understand why she was making such a big deal about it.

"If you ask me she has the patience of a saint—"

At this point I tried to ask Lea what Prue meant. Six years of what? But Lea told me to be quiet.

"I can't say I entirely blame her," Prue said.

"Fuck you," Father said.

"Oh come on," Prue said.

We listened to Prue's footsteps as she sauntered down the

corridor, then Lea followed her. I went to find Adriana in the laundry room. She let me help her pour in the detergent, which had the most delicious scent. It left the sheets delicately perfumed. She complained that she did not like her new schedule, having to stay in the evenings to serve dinner. She liked to get home to her Michelino. "Why don't you tell them to get their own food?" I suggested, and she laughed. As she leaned into the dryer for clothes, a button popped off her shirt. "It's the second time today," she said. "I don't understand why God gave me such a large bosom. I think it's a mistake." She spoke about God so familiarly, as if he were a good friend.

Neither the Ashtons nor Lea appeared for dinner. Adriana had placed the melon and prosciutto on the table. The white bubbly Lambrusco wine had been opened. Father and I were seated, waiting for them to appear. "Go and see what's taking so long," Father said.

The door to the Ashtons' room was ajar. Lea lay on the bed, laughing hysterically as Mrs. Ashton, who was bent over the bed, tickled her. Lea kept saying, "Stop, stop," trying to escape from the bed, but Mrs. Ashton kept pushing her down and continuing to tickle her. Mr. Ashton stood holding on to one of the bedposts with his back to me. He did not turn. At last, Lea screamed, "I'm going to pee in my pants if you don't stop." She threw Prue off and raced out the door, almost knocking me over. She ran down the corridor and I followed her.

Her face was flushed, her hair tangled. She lurched onto her seat. Then she raised her arm to place it around Father but her elbow knocked his glass of wine over. "Shit," he said. Lea sprinkled salt on the tablecloth.

There was an awkward silence as the Ashtons took their places.

The wind blew, rattling the shutters and the glass panes. The wind sounded different, sometimes like a soft whispering, the sound of leaves brushing against each other, at other times like a bird whistling at a higher pitch, as if the air were being sucked down a channel.

"You would think that the wind would refresh but instead—" Prue said, placing one hand to her forehead. "A frightful migraine."

Adriana brought out the soufflé, which appeared slightly burned on the exterior, but when Prue cut into it, lifting a spoonful to her plate, the melted cheese dripped onto the tablecloth.

"I think it needs a few more minutes," Prue said.

"Cook your own goddamn soufflé," Father said.

Prue placed her hand on Father's arm. For a moment, it looked as if he would move his arm away, or even hit her, but he left it there. I wondered if Father was angry with Prue for not getting Mother to return or if it was because of their exchange earlier.

Mr. Ashton said that he liked the soufflé crust burned. It was more tasty that way. He placed his napkin into the top of his shirt and told us to do the same, but Lea did not follow his example so I did not either.

The conversation was strained despite Prue's efforts. She remarked that everyone seemed related on the island. The woman who waxed her legs, Signora Martini, was a distant

66

cousin of Adriana's. Prue said that Signora Martini had given her a long lecture about how hairy people were these days. Our generation was not hairy like this generation, the Signora had said.

By the time dinner was finished, everyone was a little tipsy. Prue suggested Lea mimic the adults. Father said he thought it was getting late. We ought to be getting to bed. Lea begged him to let us stay. She lay down on the floor by his feet.

"Please, please," she said.

"Oh do get up. Really, Lea," Father said.

"Come on," Prue said. "She can start with me." Immediately, Lea sauntered across the room, pressing her palm to her forehead. She said, "Oh my dear. This wind. This wind." The Ashtons laughed. By the time Lea said, "Certainly not my idea of paradise. Just sand and more sand and wind," I was laughing hysterically. Only Father remained unmoved. I remember the look on Lea's face when she realized that he was not laughing. He was playing with the pale yellow wax that had enveloped the Pecorino cheese we had eaten at dinner. He had molded the wax into a small boat, fashioning first the hull then the sail. Lea asked if she could see it and he gave it to her and she squashed it between her fingers. "That's not very nice," Father said. "It's time for bed."

8

In the morning the sunlight colored one wall of our room, illuminating the mahogany chest of drawers, my clothes thrown over the chair. Slowly I swung my legs over the side of my bed. I did not step into my slippers because Lea complained that the sound awakened her if I scuffed down the steps leading to the second level of our bedroom. I was about to step into the bathroom when I heard voices coming from the garden. The wind seemed to have abated. It was still early and the birds sang loudly. The birds were the same color as the bushes so that the bushes themselves seemed to flutter. I went down a path only to realize that the voices came from the opposite direction, on the other side of the villa.

I saw Father first. The light touched the back of his head, revealing a perfect round circle where his hair was thinning. He was wearing Mother's favorite shirt of his, a pale blue shirt Mother said brought out the color of his eyes. Maybe he was going to visit her. He partially blocked my view of the person he was speaking to. The trouser leg splashed with paint was enough to identify Mr. Peters, however. The shoe without laces unmistakable.

Father said something I could not make out. He sounded angry, impatient to get rid of him.

Mr. Peters stepped aside, pushing back his dirty blond hair from his forehead, squinting because the sunlight was in his eyes.

I expected Father to reach into his trouser pocket for his silver clip, to slip a few bills. I had seen him do this on several occasions in the past. But all he did was glance at his watch. "I have an appointment," he said, and Mr. Peters slunk off, dragging his feet, brushing against the branches of the bush behind which I was hiding, his shoes scraping the tiles.

Father stood for a moment staring at the garden before turning and racing up to the parking lot. He did not seem to notice the sprinklers. He did not pause to time his passage. As soon as he had passed, the sprinklers wet the path.

I turned and ran straight into Mr. Ashton, who appeared from behind a bush. "Whoa," he cried as we collided. I felt his binoculars against my forehead. He had a second pair. I could smell the soap he used, a strong deodorant soap. He had brought several bars of it, obviously not trusting the island's provisions. He apologized profusely then said he had been looking for me and Lea. He had found a nest with tiny eggs he thought we might like to see. I said, "Thanks, but I want to say good-bye to Dad."

In my haste to catch up with my father, I got caught in the stream of the sprinklers. I raced up the steps to the parking lot and was just in time to say good-bye.

"I've got to go to Rome today," Father said, leaning out the window. "I'll be back by dinner." I looked inside the Jeep for his briefcase. It was not there. I raised one arm self-consciously to wave good-bye.

Wanting to tell Lea about Father and Mr. Peters, I deliberately slammed the drawers to our chest closed. I sat down beside Lea and passed my hand through her hair. But she continued to sleep.

I stepped out onto the patio and placed my damp clothes flat on the tiles. Later, Adriana scolded me, because they came away faintly yellow from the dust.

It was only when Prue called for Lea from our doorway that Lea awakened. "Coming," Lea shouted, jumping out of bed, pulling on the pink dress she had worn the day before.

At breakfast Lea and Prue ate mangoes she had bought at a stand on the road. She offered me a piece, but I did not like the texture. Lea sucked the core, juice dripping down her chin.

After breakfast, Lea and Prue played honeymoon bridge, while I drew all the objects in the living room in one corner—the glass table with its black wheels, the old model sailboat on the mantelpiece, the jar filled with the faded shells of sea urchins, even the long sofa made out of stone. The shutters were closed against the wind and the sand, the only light filtering between the blinds in oblique lines. Lea's pale pink dress seemed to reflect Prue's orange silk dress. I recall looking up and noticing Lea caressing the hem of Prue's dress.

"Did you really own a monkey?" Lea asked Prue.

"Yes, I did," she said. "His name was Claudius."

"What a funny name," Lea said.

Prue told Lea that she used to dress the monkey up in a white and blue sailor suit, a matching beret, and a red pom-pom. She said it even had its own bed, a cradle she had bought. She had trained it to use a regular toilet. Then one day, as she was lying in bed, it suddenly bit off a tiny piece of her ear. Prue touched her earlobe. But she hadn't had the heart to put it to sleep. She wouldn't have been able to bring herself to kill it, even when it bit her a second time. Poor Mr. Ashton had been forced to take care of it.

Lea asked if she had got the monkey before or after her marriage.

"Before," Mrs. Ashton said. "In fact, I remember telling Mr. Ashton it was either me and my monkey or no one."

Lea and I laughed at that.

They continued to talk with each other but now in whispers. "It's rude to whisper," I said, and Prue told me to come over and she would whisper something in my ear, but I took up my drawing again, slowly outlining the blinds. I did not notice Prue sidling over. Feeling her peer over my shoulder, I turned the picture over. "Too late," she said. "I saw it. You're a very good drawer; maybe you'll be a painter someday." Though I suspected her of flattery, I flushed with pleasure. I took special care drawing the vase, in case she came back to look. I did not notice them leaving the room.

Later, I plodded down the corridor, my drawing in one hand, past the rare prints of flowers with their water-stained paper. Adriana had told me about a particularly bad storm the winter before. Whole beaches had been ripped out. Houses swept away. The caretaker of one villa had awakened to find his mattress floating down a hallway. I liked to imagine the man with a long old-fashioned nightdress and nightcap drifting down a river.

Still holding my drawing, I stopped at the Ashtons' door. I peered through a crack. Lea and Mrs. Ashton were lying side by side on the bed. They were smoking. Too shy to knock, I turned away, stepping onto the veranda. My drawing slipped from my fingers. It flew across the garden, disappearing behind bushes. I ran after it but the wind kept blowing it farther—at last I caught it but by then it was covered with dust. I cried desperately.

I knew that what I was crying about was much larger than just a drawing. I sat on the veranda and watched the shadow of a gecko, a giant lizard, reflected onto the tiles. Dust and leaves whirled up from the dry garden. I caught sight of Mr. Ashton, just the top of his head, and I raced back inside.

I found Adriana at her ironing board. She was ironing one of Prue's dresses. She complained that the Ashtons had brought three suitcases full of dirty clothes. How was she supposed to make their bed when they never left their room? Some people were really strange, she said. Imagine! Prue had asked her to place blue, white, or pink toilet paper in their bathroom, but not yellow.

I followed Adriana as she did her chores. She allowed me to help her make the beds, fold sheets and towels, sort Father's socks into pairs. I helped her roll the gnocchi. At lunch she sent me for Prue and Lea. I knocked and the door opened a crack, revealing no one. They had left the room.

"Off with no lunch?" Adriana said. "What does this mean?"

Mr. Ashton was already at the table.

I kept my gaze on my soup, seeing no more of him than the white napkin he had tucked into the top of his shirt.

"It seems as if it's just the two of us," he said.

A silence ensued.

He tried to make conversation, but I answered in mono-syllables. He wanted to know if I liked school. I said no but would not explain why. He wanted to know if I had any boyfriends. To this question, I would not reply. At last, he sighed and then said, "I never was very good at talking to children."

"I'm not very good at talking to grown-ups," I said, feeling sorry for him. I remembered Mother saying that he was shy. That was why he had trouble looking people in the eye.

"I suppose what they talk about must seem boring," he said.

"Yes, but I do like hearing about the naughty things Mum and Prue did when they were children."

"From what I understand your Mother has always been very good," he said.

"What about you?" I asked.

"I was a very good boy," he said. "Probably too good. I had a brother—well, that's a long story. Do you mind if I smoke?"

"Oh no," I said, wanting to imitate Lea's debonair manner. In truth, I did not like the scent because it was too strong.

He offered to play cards, not bridge but gin rummy, and we played a few games beneath the pergola. I was impressed by the way he shuffled cards, and he spent some time teaching me. While I practiced shuffling, Mr. Ashton peeled one fig after the next, popping them whole into his mouth. At last, I excused myself, leaving him alone on the veranda.

I ran to Mr. Peters's villa. I stared through the shutters of one window. At first it was too dark for me to distinguish anything more than the light filtering through the cracks in the shutters, crisscrossing the room, illuminating a green plant, the corner of a painting. Gradually, however, my eyes grew accustomed to the dark and I made out two naked figures lying on the couch. Mr. Peters lay on his back, his mouth half open and letting out a snore, the woman, whom I did not recognize at first, half on top of him, her face hidden. The light illuminated her fine blond hair. For a moment, I imagined that it was Lea sleeping with Mr. Peters, because the figure was almost identical to hers, even to the shape of her long slim legs with narrow ankles, and because I did not want to acknowledge that it was Mother.

Even when I realized it was Mother, I did not admit it to myself. I marched along the outside of the painter's villa, in the wind and the sand, banging the walls and the blinds with a stick, singing some song I had learned in camp. "Un kilometre à pied ça use, ça use. Un kilometre à pied ça use les souliers." But when Mr. Peters appeared in the doorway, a towel wrapped around his waist, I ran away. Again, I desperately wanted to tell Lea about what I had seen. I knocked on the Ashtons' door. There was no answer. I knocked again.

At dinner Lea was attentive to Prue's every need. She filled her glass with wine, passed her bread, even spread butter on her roll. I tried to kick Lea under the table to get her attention. But she just ignored me. She hardly ate she was so intent on catching every word Prue uttered. Prue seemed unmoved by the attention, as if it were not unusual for her to have young girls dote on her. Father had returned in an excellent mood and asked me if I would like to have my bread buttered. "A glass of wine?" he asked. Lea scowled at him, pinching me under the table when I laughed. Father seemed determined to be pleasant and changed the subject. The Piazza di Spagna! Keats's house. After he died the whole apartment had to be fumigated. Mr. Ashton explained to Lea and me his line of business. He worked for a company that sold paint. Not any kind of paint. Special paint that was used for corking boats. While Mr. Ashton tried to engage our attention, Father leaned over and asked Prue, "How did the visit go?"

"What is the point?" she asked, talking with a facetious tone, folding her napkin in two. "When you will not reform."

"Excuse me," Father said, "I did not invite you here to moralize."

"I was just joking," Prue said. "As a matter of fact she was out."

I knew where she had been.

"I see," Father said.

"You cannot have your pie and eat it too," she said.

"Why not?" Father asked.

"Then don't agonize so much about it. Have fun. Have a ball."

Father laughed.

"You would make my job a little easier if you were more discreet."

"She is not particularly discreet either. Anyway, now we're even."

"I'm afraid it doesn't always work that way," Mr. Ashton interjected.

I understood very little of this conversation. How Father

needed to reform was not clear. Perhaps Prue was referring to his temper. I am sure that Lea understood everything. She was a teenager, while I was still a child.

I had to wait all evening, late into the night, before I finally got Lea alone. I climbed into her bed and she asked me if I had had a bad dream.

"I saw Mr. Peters and Mum on the couch," I said.

"Oh," Lea said. "I knew about that."

She lifted one arm so that her hand cut the path of the moonlight filtering through the curtains then let her hand drop.

"Prue doesn't like to use yellow toilet paper," I said.

"So what?" she said. "She tells me ev-er-y-thing." She pronounced each syllable separately for extra emphasis. "I mean things you wouldn't even know about—"

"Like what?"

"Like her first sexual experience. She was only twelve. She just wanted to get it done and over with. She didn't care who she did it with."

"Wow." I couldn't help being impressed.

"And—you swear not to tell anyone?"

"I promise."

"She says her husband's a bad lover."

"She didn't," I said.

"She did. I swear."

"No."

We laughed but I thought it was mean of Prue to say that about her husband. I knew better than to share this thought with Lea, however. I no longer knew how she would respond to anything. What I took to be strange, like Mother sleeping with Mr. Peters, Lea seemed to find quite normal, while she seemed to find amusing the fact that Mr. Ashton was a bad lover.

9

The wind continued to blow. No longer the cool mistral from the north, but the hot sirocco from Africa. A thin layer of dust covered plates, glasses, books, and even our toothbrushes the next morning. Some of the pine trees were missing branches. Passing the Ashtons' room, I caught a glimpse through the half-open curtains of a glinting silver tray. I heard Mr. Ashton complain about crumbs in his bed.

I went in search of Adriana, finding her in our bedroom, where she complained that our beds were impossible to make. They were composed of wood boxes placed on bases that had been carved out of the island rock, and the mattresses fit tightly inside the boxes so that there was barely enough room to tuck in the sheets. I tried to help Adriana pull the sheet over one corner. Down one side she found Lea's gold watch. Then I heard footsteps I recognized. I let go of the mattress and peered over the side to the lower level.

Mother stood in a beam of light. She wore a lime-colored dress she had worn the day Lea and I had seen her talking to Mr. Peters.

I tread carefully down the steep stairs, counting the steps. When she looked up, Mother held out a small packet wrapped in gold paper. "One is for you, and one is for Lea," she said. Inside the box, I found a coral necklace. As Mother leaned over to fasten the clasp, her hair fell on my shoulder and I remembered the smell and held her tight. I would not let go. "Let go of me," she said and laughed, gently unclasping my hands from around her neck. "I'm so glad to be back. I missed you."

I bunched up the skirt of my dress in one hand then tried to smooth out the creases.

"Where's Lea?" Mother asked.

"Probably with Prue," I said, following Mother out into the garden.

"Have they become great friends?" Mother asked.

"Yes," I said.

"I thought they would," she said. "And what about you?" She took my hand.

I pulled her toward the hammock, hoping to have a moment alone with her, but Prue and Lea stepped out of the path.

Mother and Prue stood facing one another, the skirts of their dresses flapping in the wind. Mother held hers down with one hand while Prue allowed hers to open, revealing her long tanned legs.

Then Mother embraced Prue very tight. "I'm so glad you're here," she said.

"I'm so glad you decided to come back," Prue said.

Lea stepped from behind her. She said hello, keeping her hands clasped behind her back.

Mother held out a gold packet, but Lea just slipped it into her pocket without opening it.

"Aren't you going to give me a hug?" Mother asked. "I missed you so much." She tried to hug Lea but she stood with her arms by her sides.

"We're going to make sachets," Lea said. "Prue bought some in Arzachena yesterday."

"We'll do that later," Prue said, taking Mother's arm. "Your mother and I have some catching up to do."

Lea and I watched them walk down the path, arm over arm. Mother glanced back at us once and shouted something like "I won't be long."

Lea climbed into the hammock. She swung very fast then she asked, "What are you staring at?"

"Nothing," I said.

Later Lea and I peered through the wood shutters of the Ashtons' room, getting a fright. Prue and Mother had covered their faces with what looked like green mud. Mother was lying with her head hanging over the side of the bed. Prue smoked as she reclined against a pillow.

"Do you remember poor Miss—" Prue said.

"We were so awful," Mother said. "Cruel—"

"But she deserved it," Prue said, then leaned over and said something I could not make out, which made Mother laugh.

"I haven't laughed so hard in a long time," Mother said.

"I haven't either," Prue said. "Not since your honeymoon. Do you remember how we used to laugh?"

Lea told me that Prue had accompanied Mum and Dad on their honeymoon, but in Spain Prue had fallen in love with a bullfighter and run off with him. Mum had told me that story too, only I remembered the part about Prue lying in the sun to bronze herself for the bullfighter but ending up instead burning herself so completely she was *cramoisie*. Mother had used the French word, and even as a child it seemed to me so much more evocative than the word *burned*.

"Doesn't that seem like a long time ago?" Prue said.

"Yes," Mother said. "I feel old."

"But you look about twenty," Prue said. "And thirty-five is hardly old."

"It's not young anymore," Mother said.

"I'm so glad you decided to come back. What made you change your mind? It couldn't have been just to see me."

"I missed the girls," Mother said. "He says he's going to be good."

"I'm sure he's said that before," Prue said.

"Yes," she said. "But he's never promised to break it off."

"Ah," Prue said, extending one arm toward the ashtray on the bedside table.

Eventually they emerged from Prue's room, traces of the green masks still visible around the line of their hair. Mother went to her room, while Prue set us to work at the dining room table, sewing sachets and filling them with rosemary and thyme.

"What were you and Mum talking about?" Lea asked.

"Wouldn't you like to know," Prue said. She leaned over and prodded Lea in the ribs.

"Don't," Lea said, but laughed.

"Things," Prue said, putting on a young girl's voice, pretending to chew gum. "Boys—"

Lea and I laughed.

Then Prue leaned forward and slipped an ice cube down the front of Lea's dress and Lea stood up and dropped one down her dress and Prue screamed then dropped one down mine and we laughed. She told us about the midnight feasts she and Mother used to have in boarding school—sardines, yogurt, and candy, and Lea begged her to have a midnight feast with us. "We'll see. We'll see," she said. She told us how she used to tell stories all night long until all the girls fell asleep.

Prue suggested going for a walk. I did not know whether I was invited or not. I can see myself standing beneath the archway of stones, watching them make their way down the hill toward the Piccolo Pevero beach. Then I followed.

When I reached the beach, it was deserted, just footsteps already half erased leading to dunes. Every now and then the wind would blow and sand would fly up and whip my legs and arms. The sea seemed the exact color of the sky, so that it was almost impossible to distinguish the two. They were not swimming. I thought they might have crossed over to the other beach, so I climbed several steep hills, stopping from time to time to remove pebbles from my red sneakers. Hardly anyone used this path.

As I approached the top of a hill, I heard voices. I caught sight of Prue and Lea pirouetting down the path, their brown bodies outlined against the sun. All they wore were shoes. They skipped and twirled and shouted and laughed and then they ran. I wanted to tell them to stop, to wait for me.

But then I realized I was not the only onlooker. Standing on the other side of the path, partially hidden by a bush, was Mr. Ashton, fully clothed, his hands in his pockets. Mother had drawn my attention to this habit of his. I felt sorry for him, imagining that he felt the same way I did about Lea and Prue's friendship.

After witnessing this scene, I ran home. I planned to tell Mother. But when I arrived, she was in the kitchen stirring tomato sauce, while Father stood cutting basil. This scene of quiet domesticity was so unusual in our household that I did not feel up to disrupting it. Furthermore, I wondered if they would believe me. Perhaps they would mock me. "Prue and Lea dancing in the nude while Mr. Ashton watched?" I imagined Father saying. I remember Father placing his hand on my head, in a rare gesture of affection.

10

The remarkable harmony extended over the following days. The wind continued to blow, but no one, except for Adriana and me, seemed to mind. At one end of the villa, Mother and Father spent their time in their bedroom. At the other end of the villa, Prue and Lea played cards. Mr. Ashton was either in his room or staggering about in the wind.

I spent most of my time alone. Sometimes, I played with Carla, Adriana's niece. We played older sister and younger sister. I was the older sister in the game, Carla the younger. Carla had to do what I told her to do. I made her march in the wind and the dust along the wall of the garden. I forced her to eat dirt as Lea had once made me, the promise of a Cinderella doll enough to silence her.

One afternoon, at the end of a day of being confined to the villa and its garden, I passed the Ashtons' room. I had nothing planned. The shutters were ajar. The sun fell directly on the top of Prue's chest of drawers, highlighting the pillboxes. I glanced around, and seeing no one, snuck inside and slipped the green emerald box I had admired before into my pocket. Where to hide it? I concealed it in the secret cache where Lea placed her belongings, under a loose tile in our bedroom.

I have no doubt that I hid it there to get Lea into trouble, though at the time I would have denied it.

All afternoon, I waited for Prue or Lea to say something, but there was no mention of it. Observing how Prue and Lea stopped talking when I drew near them, I imagined that they knew.

It wasn't until evening that the topic was brought up. Prue and Mother were sitting in the living room, drinking gin and tonics.

Lea came skipping into the room. She had just taken a shower and her hair was still damp. She threw herself onto the couch beside Prue.

"If there's one thing I hate, it's dishonesty," Prue said, enunciating each word clearly and moving away from Lea.

I felt that she was directing her words to me, though it was clear she was talking to Lea.

"Where did you put it?" Prue asked Lea.

"What?" Lea asked.

"Surely there's been a mistake," Mother said.

"And it's not the first time," Prue said.

"I don't know what you mean," Lea said, standing with her hands on her hips, but her face turned crimson.

"Don't pretend," Prue said. "The pillboxes."

"Perhaps we should ask Adriana," Mother suggested. "Adriana."

"Yes," Adriana answered, standing with her feet apart, firmly planted. Despite her stature, she projected an impression of strength.

"Have you by any chance seen Mrs. Ashton's pillboxes—"

"A green one and a pale blue one in the shape of an egg," Prue said.

"No," Adriana said, looking put out, as if Mother were implying that she had stolen them. She marched down the corridor while we waited in silence.

I should have told the truth, but I could not bring myself to. I prayed that Adriana would not find the two boxes.

When she returned, she held them in her hand.

"Is this what you are looking for?" she asked.

I felt my own face flush. I could not say a word.

"I didn't take the green one," Lea said.

"But you took the other," Prue said.

"I'm so ashamed," Mother said. "I don't know what to say, Prue. Lea, you're to apologize immediately."

Lea glanced at me with utter contempt. She slipped out into the garden despite the wind, while I slunk back down the corridor to our room. At the time, I felt completely responsible for the misunderstanding between Prue and Lea.

The grown-ups planned to take us out for dinner that evening. But when Mother called for us, Lea still hadn't reappeared. I didn't dare say anything. We all got into the Jeep. The wind blew, rattling the glass panes of the Jeep.

"What's taking Lea so long?" Father asked.

"I'm sure she'll be here any minute," Mother said.

"Helen, go see what she's doing," Father said.

I climbed out. The wind blew the door to the villa shut behind me. Inside it was quiet. I stood for a moment taking in the living room with its red tiles, the sofas with their orange covers with embroidered flowers, before stepping out onto the veranda. Just the sound of bougainvillea, like crepe paper, brushing back and forth across the patio. Some had got tangled in the hem of the thick cream curtain. Then I heard weeping.

Lea sat on the steps, her head in her arms.

I ambled over. "Why are you crying?"

"I'm not," Lea said, wiping her eyes with her sleeve.

I reached out to touch her shoulder, but she shrugged my hand off. I sat down beside her as she stretched out her legs. They were badly scratched. She ran her finger along a particularly deep scratch.

"They're waiting," I said.

"I don't care," she said.

"Girls," we heard Mother call.

"Shit," Lea said.

"Shit," I said.

"It's all your fault," she said.

"I'm sorry," I said.

"I'm sorry," she said, imitating my tone of voice, mocking my contrition. "What good does that do me? You've ruined everything."

In the Jeep I kept glancing in the rearview mirror at Lea, who sat pressed against the side window. At one point, Lea started to roll down the window, but Prue said, "Oh please!"

Clouds of dust rose on either side of the Jeep so that we could see only what was directly before us, glimpses of the green golf course, a sliver of blue water, and then more dust and stone walls.

The hotel, like many of the villas, was painted white. With its numerous turrets it looked like some enchanted castle, and in the dying sunlight, the pink and purple bougainvillea appeared fluorescent.

When we arrived, Mr. Ashton helped Prue get down from the Jeep. Lea jumped down but trailed behind. She paused to pluck clovers.

"Do you want me to help you?" I asked. Lea shrugged and Father turned and told us to hurry. I ran up ahead.

The restaurant stood on a beach; a wall of glass separated us from the sea and the sand. Perhaps this feature explained its popularity that night. It afforded people their closest contact with the beach. The restaurant had been designed to resemble a boat. The back wall had portholes instead of windows, and miniature hulls without sails affixed to it.

I always found the wait between courses long, but that night it seemed interminable. The restaurant was understaffed, with each waiter responsible for a dozen tables. At the same time, there seemed to be a large number of busboys standing around, as if they had been assigned specific tasks from which they could not swerve. I dropped my napkin twice, and twice it was replaced.

When at last they brought the fish, the waiter placed the wrong kind on my plate. I would have said nothing but Lea exclaimed, "She didn't order that."

"It's okay," I said.

"No, no," Father said. "You should have what you ordered. Send it back."

"If she doesn't mind," Mother said.

The maître d' said that it was my accent. I had whispered. He had not understood.

"Some nerve," Father said, "to blame it on her."

"Perhaps she did say it incorrectly," Prue said.

"She said it like everybody else," Lea said.

I flushed with pleasure at Lea taking my defense, but then catching the angry look Lea gave Prue I realized that it was said probably more for Prue's benefit.

"I have a feeling the wind will drop tonight," Mother said.

"Let's hope so," Father said.

"Perhaps we could all go on a picnic," Prue said.

"What a lovely idea!" Mother said.

"I don't know," Father said. "Sand and flies in your food!"

"I hate picnics," I heard Lea whisper.

Lea tapped the leg of the table with her foot. She plucked one of the yellow flowers from the vase at the center of the table and slowly tore off the petals, streaking the cloth with orange pistil. "Look," she said, glancing up toward the door, "Mr. Peters." Lea and I caught sight of him before the grown-ups. We watched him stagger unsteadily across the floor. We had never seen him so dressed up. He wore a navy blue suit with a white shirt, a gold clip holding a blue tie with green stripes into place. He even wore a new pair of glasses, which reflected the light.

"Hi," he said, in a loud voice that caused several people to turn. He drew up a chair from another table without asking, sitting down between Mother and Prue. He played with the butter knife, running the edge across the white tablecloth.

There was an awkward silence. A busboy came round to fill our glasses with water.

"I have something to tell you," Mr. Peters said.

Everyone at the table turned to look at him. He opened his mouth but then closed it. He lifted Mother's glass of wine. He played with Prue's roll.

"Is this really necessary?" Father said.

Mr. Peters pushed back his hair. He pared his nails with the butter knife.

"Lea's looking the picture of health," Father said, trying to change the topic no doubt. "Soon you'll be a young lady." Lea was looking her best, her cheeks flushed from the wind and the sand, her hair almost white. Her forehead glistened. She undid the two top buttons of her dress. The gesture was innocent. She was warm.

However, when Mother gathered the top of her own dress, a gesture that Prue understood as well, Lea became aware of what she was doing. Instead of stopping, she undid another button.

It was then Mr. Peters made his remark.

"Looking very fetching tonight," he said. "In a few years she'll be a good—"

Father stood but Mr. Ashton was quicker. I was surprised by how fast he moved. He punched Mr. Peters in the face. Mr. Peters slumped to the ground. His glasses fell off.

Suddenly, it was very quiet. Then someone coughed as Mother knelt by Mr. Peters. The maître d' strutted over to our table. He said, "Excuse me. Excuse me. I cannot have this type of behavior in my establishment."

"Don't worry," Father said. "That will be all for tonight."

The maître d' wiped his forehead with a white napkin and slunk away, glancing over his shoulder, as if to make sure we weren't up to any more mischief. He said something to the band and they began to play.

"I don't know why—" Prue said.

"He shouldn't have—" Mr. Ashton said.

"It's all Lea's fault," Prue said.

"What do you mean?" Father asked.

"You saw her," Prue said, mimicking the way Lea had unbuttoned her dress.

"Oh come on," Father said. "She's just a child." He turned to look at Lea, but she no longer sat in her chair.

"She must have gone to the loo," Mother said.

Prue put her napkin down. She rushed across the dining room floor with Mr. Ashton at her heels.

By this time Mr. Peters was seated again. His nose was bleeding and he held a white napkin to it.

Father made his way to the bar.

There was no sign of Lea.

I was left with Mother and Mr. Peters. Mother placed her arm around me, but I soon moved from under her arm and played with the candle, lifting it from the red lantern, letting wax drip across the white tablecloth in a pattern. I overheard very little of what Mother and Mr. Peters said. I kept expecting Lea to return. When the musicians paused, the sound of the sand against the glass windows became audible. Mr. Peters kept asking "Why?" while Mother kept saying,

"But you must see. Please understand." Mother kept glancing at me.

I slipped away from the table, walking down a corridor, out a door, and onto the beach.

The wind blew, whipping up the sand, stinging my legs and arms. The sea was rough, covered with small choppy waves. The wood umbrellas creaked. Two blue cushions flipped over in the sand, one blowing out onto the water. I paused to touch the sand. It was coarse, very different from the Piccolo Pevero beach. There was no sign of Lea, but in the distance, beneath the purple sky, I saw a playground, just a slide and a few swings. I loved swings.

I swung for a long time with my eyes closed against the sand and the wind.

When I got down, I noticed Mr. Ashton by the only gate. I tread self-consciously across the playground. I wondered whether Mother or Father had sent him to look for me. I whispered, "Excuse me," but he continued to lean against the gate. He smoked. The smell of his cigar was very strong and sweet. He inhaled deeply and exhaled slowly. The ashes blew onto my hair. His brown hair was parted to the side and neatly plastered down.

"Have you seen Lea?" he asked. Prue must have sent him to find Lea. She was always sending him on errands.

"No," I said, looking down at the sand. I smoothed it with my shoe. Sand slipped into my patent leather shoe and later I felt its weight as I scrambled through the garden of the hotel.

"Will you help me find her?" he said.

"All right," I said.

He opened the gate and I followed him. He walked fast, very fast, taking tiny steps. I had to walk more and more quickly, until I almost ran, up a path of flattened stones, in and out of African daisies and torch lilies flattened by the wind, over to a place where many streams crossed, beyond a patch of clover, up worn yellow stairs leading to a side entrance of the hotel.

I paused to glance back at the restaurant. The sound of the music was faint. After the brilliant sunset, the interior of the hotel seemed cool and shadowy, the empty ballroom, in which I now found myself, cold and dark, so different from the restaurant filled with light, with the clatter of knives and forks against porcelain. The ballroom was filled with shadows, tables arranged against one wall, only one chandelier half lit by the last ray of sun slipping through a pair of dark velvet curtains. The rug was so thick that I could not hear my own footsteps. The ceiling seemed exceedingly high. I followed Mr. Ashton into the ladies' room. He called for Lea. He stopped in front of a mirror, running a small black comb through his hair without touching the parting. It was then I realized that something was wrong, only I felt it was too late to do anything about it. He pulled me into a stall. I heard a loud click as the door locked, his hands around my neck. "I'll strangle you, if you call out," he said. I did not cry out. I did what he told me to do. I took off the green dress and matching underwear. I stood with my body bent, arms wrapped around my chest. I tried to keep my eyes on the pink tiles as he put up the toilet lid and sat down. I thought he was going to the bathroom. I listened to the creaking of the toilet seat. When I looked up, I saw white liquid glistening from his penis. I thought that he was sick, then stared at the pink tiled floor again. I saw a fleck of red lipstick on the floor. "You wait here," he said. "And not a word to anyone. This is our secret." I continued to look down, heard the door to the stall close. I listened to him cross the bathroom, the sound of sand being ground into the tile, like chalk squeaking across a blackboard.

At last, all was silent and I pulled on my underwear, my dress, then stared through the half-open door. I waited a little longer, what seemed like a long time but was probably no more than five or ten minutes. I feared he might be hiding behind a door, a column. At last, I could wait no longer and ran as fast as I could through the entrance hall, where I almost collided into an elegant woman whose hair was done up in a chignon. I ran down the steps, through the garden, along the beach, all the way to the restaurant, where the Ashtons were dancing as if nothing had happened. Lea stood at the buffet nibbling a chocolate eclair. Mother and Father sat opposite each other at the table. On my plate lay a silver fish, its glazed eye reflecting the candlelight.

Father slapped the table and Mother jumped back.

"I hate it when you're like this," she said.

"And I hate it—" Father said.

"There's nothing," Mother started, I couldn't hear the rest. Their voices were faint.

I stood by the table noticing a stain in the white tablecloth. The glass still lay on its side. But no one seemed to notice it and I wondered whether or not to stand it up straight. Mother glanced over at me and motioned for me to come over but they looked so angry with each other, I went over to Lea standing by the buffet table, where the food displayed—the prosciutto and melon, the mozzarella and tomatoes, and the orange centers of the black mussels, which glistened in the now dim light—no longer looked appetizing.

I placed my arms around Lea's waist, rested my cheek against her chest.

On the return route I lay beside Lea in the back of the Jeep on the floor. I noticed that the windows of a church, which appeared yellow in the day, were now black. I pretended that we were on a train in our own separate compartment.

"Prue," Mr. Ashton said, his voice contrite.

"You're really getting tiresome," Prue said.

"But that—"

"Please," Mother said. "Oh please."

"If you say that one more time I'm going to—" Father said.

"If you had listened," Prue said.

"Oh shut up," Father said.

I did not know what they were talking about. I did not care. I could not bear the sound of Mr. Ashton's voice, knowing that he was only a few feet away from me. I focused on the moon slipping in and out of the clouds, a trail of mist in its wake like a tail. It looked like a snake to me, while Lea thought it looked like an egg.

Later that night I awakened. The room changed from light to dark as the moon moved in and out of the clouds. Lea's bed, with its white sheets thrown back, appeared then disappeared. Windows shuddered in their hinges, dry leaves brushed the floor, and in the distance the wind sounded like the sea. From time to time, when the wind abated, I could hear the cicadas. I got out of bed and crossed over to the window. I stared at the moon's reflection on the sea. I felt distant, as if I were the moon looking in on me. I remember getting into Lea's bed, her warm body next to mine.

11

Over the following days the atmosphere in the villa was very tense; when the Ashtons weren't fighting, our parents were, as if our dinner had blown away what feeble restraints had been in place. Each morning the wind started to blow, gathering strength in the afternoon, and by evening it raged. Trees were whipped and sand flew through the air. Now and then we would hear a branch crack, a tree felled. I had the impression of being on a boat tossed about at sea. We were confined to the villa. The Ashtons rarely stepped over the threshold of their room. Our parents and the Ashtons spoke in monosyllables to each other.

I was probably the only one gladdened by these tensions. But I could not escape Mr. Ashton's presence altogether. A draft would carry the sweet, nauseating smell of his cigar into our room. Hearing his footsteps, I would hide in the walk-in closet in our bedroom.

Lea and I were thrown together, but she refused to talk to me. She was still angry. Ordinarily, I would have tried to coax her out of her bad humor, but I felt strangely apathetic. After what had happened, her concerns seemed unimportant.

I became obsessed with a painting hanging in our bedroom.

Father had once told us that the painter had done it while in prison. This had never bothered me before, but now I found myself attracted and repulsed by it, though the subject matter, ostensibly, was not frightening: an albino donkey against a rocky landscape similar to Bella Terra's. The donkey's head was turned as if he were expecting someone, but there was no one. I felt its shadow was not in the right place. It seemed to me that it should be in front of him instead of in back. I sat for hours staring at the painting, while Lea sat on her bed, her back turned to me. On one occasion, she looked in her secret cache. "I'll kill you if you go into this one," she said.

"I won't. I promise I won't," I said.

"That's what you said last time," she said. "I can't trust you."

"You can. You can," I said, and I meant to keep to my word. I always did but sometimes I could not help peeking, feeling that this was the only way to read her secret thoughts.

Lea turned onto her back, hands folded beneath her head.

"I can't wait to be a grown-up," she said.

"Why?"

"Because then I can travel round the world," she said. "I can do what I want."

"But you already do what you want," I said. "I don't think I ever want to grow up."

This was the longest conversation we had had in several days. I sidled over to her bed.

"Lea," I said.

"Yes," she said.

I was about to climb up onto her bed when she gave me one of her looks. I would have liked to lie beside her, to rest my head on her shoulder.

"Nothing," I said. I could not bring myself to tell her about Mr. Ashton.

I might have found comfort with Mother, but she spent much of her time behind closed doors. One evening, taking a bath with her, I contemplated telling her what had happened, when she remarked that she sometimes wished she could be a child again. Wouldn't it be nice to have no responsibilities, no preoccupations beyond whether or not the wind would stop blowing so that we could go to the beach? She said she was sure that I would soon get breasts. She had got her period at eleven. I remember thinking that I did not want breasts. I would prefer to remain completely flat like a boy.

Strangely enough, it was Prue I came closest to telling. Father and Mr. Ashton had gone shopping and I was drifting desultorily down the narrow hallway, counting the number of tiles, when I happened to notice her door ajar. She was sitting at her table, not looking at herself, but at photographs. She placed them in a drawer when I peered in.

"Hello, you," she said, turning.

"Hello," I said, continuing to stand just outside her door.

"Come on in."

I entered her room, stood by her bed, holding on to one bedpost.

"What have you been up to?" she asked.

"Nothing," I said. "What were those photos of?"

"Me," Prue said. "Come and see."

She spread photos of herself across the table. I hardly recognized her. In one, she was completely bald. In another, her hair was cut short and she looked like a boy. She laughed at my expression then slid them back into the drawer.

I would have liked to examine them more carefully.

"So what do you have to say for yourself?" She stared at me playfully and for a moment I felt I understood why Lea liked Prue so much.

"I took the other pillbox," I said.

"Oh, I figured that out long ago," she said, pulling one side of her long white skirt over the other.

"But you're still mad with Lea," I asked.

"Is that what she says?"

"No, but I thought so."

"Sometimes things are more complicated than they seem," she added mysteriously. She told me about having a friend once whom she adored, following her everywhere she went, mimicking everything she did, until at last her friend told her to go away, never to come back. "I was so crushed at the time, but I suppose I was boring."

Lea often called me boring but I knew Prue was not referring to my relationship with Lea.

"You mean Lea is like that," I said.

"Something along those lines," she said.

"I met someone," I said. "On the beach." I stared into her eyes for some glimmer of recognition but they remained uncomprehending. Then I grew afraid of having said too much.

"Who?" she asked, twisting her long hair back into a bun but then letting it drop.

"Nobody," I said.

"Go on. Tell me."

"No, no, no," I said.

Adriana was the only person who noticed that I was different. I recall standing in the kitchen, my forehead pressed against a glass pane, listening to the wind whistle around the house, staring at the bougainvillea swirl through the air, when she called me using the Italian version of my name, "Helenina, what is the matter?" I turned and she pressed me to her soft warm apron.

12

The next morning when I awakened, I felt something was missing. Light played across the red tiles, filtered through the curtains, highlighting the blue stripes. The pink and yellow flower pattern seemed faded. The curtains were still. The wind had stopped. The sound had been constant for so many days that I felt sure I could hear it, in the same way seashells placed to one's ear give the illusion of hearing the far-off ocean.

Voices drifted from the kitchen.

"Picnics are not my idea of fun," Father said.

"Oh come on, darling," Mother said.

"We haven't been to the beach since the day I arrived," Prue said.

"Let's," Lea said.

A few days before I would have enjoyed the prospect of a picnic at the beach, the thought of running across the sand, swimming. Now I felt only the desire to stay in the villa, in my room.

I played no part in the preparations for the picnic. I was forced to get up, but I spent my time with Lea in the small back patio that led to the kitchen, drifting from hibiscus to hibiscus, collecting the heads of flowers that had fallen during the night.

I payed attention to the grown-ups only when Adriana started to tell Lea a particularly macabre story about a man who had attempted suicide but had succeeded only in blowing off his face. Mother asked if Adriana could not think of something more cheering. "These stories are not for children," she said, and Adriana marched off to hang up the laundry and Lea and I followed her. Why had he wanted to commit suicide? Lea wanted to know. All Adriana knew was that he now lived alone up in the hills with his dog. He wore a wool mask at all times.

"Even when it's hot?" I asked.

"I say a prayer for him every night," Adriana declared.

Lea thought it would be better to be dead. But Adriana thought Lea was wrong. Adriana knew a girl who was completely paralyzed, except for her eyes and one finger. This girl had written a moving book.

Perhaps it was Adriana who suggested the Cervo beach. There was some discussion, amongst the grown-ups, right up to the last minute, about which beach we should go to. Father suggested we try a new one. He had heard of a pink beach of crushed coral. Prue wanted the Cala di Volpe beach.

Only Lea and I were indifferent. Lea was busy pressing the hibiscus she had just picked in a notebook. She showed the book to Prue but Prue said she was too busy to look at it just then. She must go lather herself with cream in preparation for the sun.

The Cervo beach seems an odd choice to me now. We could not reach it by car but had to walk all the way to the Piccolo

Pevero beach and up a steep path covered with rocks and boulders, the same path where I had caught a glimpse of Prue and Lea dancing naked. Perhaps the choice was made because the Cervo beach and the Piccolo Pevero were the two beaches best protected from the wind. Though there was not a breath of air, everyone still feared that the wind would start up again.

At the start I'm sure that everyone except for me felt a sense of release. The night before it had rained and everything sparkled. The golf course shimmered. White shorts and shirts stood out against the green lawn. The scents of the flowers were particularly pungent. I recall Lea waiting for me to catch up with her. She crushed one of the tiny white myrtle flowers between her fingers, making me sneeze, then laughed and ran ahead.

I like to hold that moment, to picture Lea again, in her white dress and the droopy white hat, her hair curling in the heat.

I felt as if I were underwater.

Prue strode far ahead, her head wrapped in a scarf, a flash of red appearing now and then above the bushes. Lea ran forward and back, from Prue to Mother and Father and me, while Mr. Ashton trailed far behind.

When we reached the first beach, the Piccolo Pevero, it was packed. The entire island seemed to have convened. You could barely see the white sand. The scent of people's suntan lotions and food pervaded the air. Father remarked that it was a good thing we were not planning to picnic here. We passed a man lying in the shade of an umbrella with two women. The man called out to Father. I did not at first recognize him as the cabdriver who had driven us from the airport. He commented on the weather, shook his finger in Father's face. Then he introduced Father to his wife and daughter. He pointed to Lea, who was already floating on her back in the sea. The water was unusually warm. I had expected to find it cold after so many windy days. "A friend of mine died from jumping in cold water," Mr. Ashton said, his voice low and quiet. I had not noticed him catch up with us. I pictured his friend jumping into the water and then floating, his clothes filled with air. I threw myself into the water, then swam as fast as I could over to Lea. I stared up at the sky. A perfect blue. Our first swim seemed to have happened so long ago. I felt no urge to search for the sea urchin shells and somehow this seemed significant.

The grown-ups were still in good humor as we crossed behind the beach along that stretch of soft sand with the yellow nettles, which had miraculously survived. Father said he had enjoyed seeing the cabdriver again. I walked between Mother and Father. Lea told them about the time we had tapped people's bums with sticks and Mother and Father laughed. "You naughty girls," Father said, but in an amused tone of voice. Then Lea ran ahead. He called after her, but she disappeared around a curve. By this time, Prue was no longer in sight either. I kept glancing back to see whether Mr. Ashton was still following us. He shuffled, looking down at his feet. He always wore leather shoes, even to go to the beach, and he never swam.

We had climbed the first hill, which was very steep, obstructed by huge boulders and rocks, when all of a sudden we heard the sound of hooves. I looked up and saw Lea standing in the middle of the path as a white horse and a black one galloped over the top of the hill. Lea stood her ground but the horses swerved around her. They came galloping toward us. Father pushed Mother and me to one side. A cloud of dust rose in the air. I caught sight of a woman on one horse with a brilliant white shirt, a man dressed in black. They tore down the hill. "Idiots," Father said, as we watched them make their way down the path, then trot along the stretch of white sand we had just crossed. In the meantime, Lea had joined us. I stared at her, searching for a mark on her pristine white dress and hat, thinking that she could not have escaped unscathed.

Although this incident had disrupted the grown-ups' mood, no one suggested we turn back, not even Mother. It was only when we reached the top of the second hill that Mother voiced her doubts. Her heart was starting to flutter, she said. She did not know if she would be able to make it all the way to the beach. Father suggested we rest for a few minutes. He hastened to point out that we were two thirds of the way there. We had only one more hill to climb and then it was all flat. The view would be worth it. Mother said she did not know if she could walk all the way back. Mr. Ashton, who had caught up with us, said that it would be cooler by then and we would take it slowly. "Anyway," Father said, "it doesn't look as if we have any choice. As usual, Lea has gone off."

"She'll soon be back," Mother said.

It must have been close to one by then and the sun was high in the sky and beat down on the brown bushes and the rocks. I wished Mr. Ashton would leave us. Whenever his gaze happened to cross mine, it went blank, as if he refused to see me. He was unusually talkative and told us that he had run into a wild boar the night before. He said he had seen its eyes glittering in the dark. He had come face to face with it. "What did you do?" I asked, without thinking. Undoubtedly because I liked the idea of him cornered by a wild boar. "I hid behind a bush," he said. He still had burrs on his trousers and shirt.

If Mr. Peters had not appeared in the distance at this point, wiping his forehead with a big white handkerchief, Mother might not have agreed to continue on. Mr. Ashton said, "Look who's followed us? A desperate case!" Mother said she felt better and allowed Mr. Ashton to hold her arm. I did not want her to hold his arm but when I protested she suggested that I hold her other arm, so I ran up to Father and held his hand. I hated seeing Mother lean on Mr. Ashton. I kept turning to see if Mr. Peters was following us. His face was bright red. Once he waved with his white handkerchief, then he disappeared. There was still no sign of Lea or Prue.

The sun was so hot I thought I smelled something burning. I longed to see the sea, and at last, coming over the third hill, we saw it, a sheet of silver in the distance, a motorboat and a water-skier like a toy boat and an ant glued to it.

We could also make out Lea, who had almost reached the bottom of the cliff. She was zigzagging back and forth.

Apart from the breathtaking view of the sea from the cliff and its protected position, the Cervo beach was the worst one in the area with only a narrow strip of sand. Wading into the water was tricky. There were hundreds and hundreds of pebbles; smooth, gray, yellow, pink, black, brown pebbles.

But the water was unbelievably clear. You could see each pebble clearly defined.

By the time we reached the beach, I felt hot, ready for another swim.

Lea stood on the jetty, ricocheting pebbles across the flat surface of the sea. Prue sat a few feet away, at the end of the jetty, her feet not quite reaching the water, her back to the beach, her head still wrapped in the scarf. I padded over to the edge of the sea, moved my foot back and forth through the water, all the time keeping my eye on Lea, noting the expression of disgust on her face when she turned away as a small motorboat entered the harbor, disrupting her game. I wanted so much to grab her hand and force her to run with me and tell her what had happened. Instead, Prue's scarf somehow floated onto the sea and sank to the bottom. Lea dived and dived in an effort to retrieve it, but it had gone down too deep.

Boats were the only vehicles that could reach the beach. Every hour a motorboat would come into the harbor from a hotel in Costa Paradiso. The beach itself was divided in half: one half servicing hotel guests, the other half open to the public. Hotels put up umbrellas and chaise longues, underneath which you could only sit if you were a guest.

I had just settled myself in the shade of one of these umbrellas, as far from Mr. Ashton as possible, when a young man with curly blond hair strode up to us and asked if we were staying at the Porto Cervo hotel. When Father informed him that we were not, the young man told us that we could not lie beneath the umbrellas. Father told him not to be ridiculous. There were three people on the beach, dozens of unused umbrellas. Mother tried to be conciliatory, "Dear, it doesn't—we can—" The young man said that these were the rules and regulations. He had not made them up. He placed his hands on his hips. Father stood, his head just missing the wood umbrella. The young man kicked the sand but not in our direction. He muttered something about having to talk to his superiors. Father said, "You do that." The outcome of this short exchange was that we stayed beneath the umbrellas but each time the motorized boat came in I feared that we might have to relinquish them.

Looking over at the jetty again, I caught sight of Lea sidling toward Prue. She reached out and touched her shoulder but Prue shrugged her off and Lea retreated back a few steps. Then Lea said something. I could not hear what. Prue stood. I could see she was angry. She said something very fast. Lea's shoulders dropped, and then she turned and ran across the dock, the beach, blowing up sand in her wake. "Attenzione, attenzione," a woman shouted. Lea disappeared into one of the changing cabins at the back of the beach.

All this time I had been lying on a chaise longue in the sun. My legs, perhaps because of the sun and the salt, were itching me terribly and I went to dip them in the water, even though I knew that the salt would only make them worse.

When I glanced back at the beach, Lea was kneeling in the shade of an umbrella, writing or drawing on a piece of paper; at that distance I could not see. Her face was obscured by the white floppy hat. She crumpled several pages, started writing on a new piece, glanced at her gold watch, resumed writing. At last she seemed satisfied and folded a piece of paper, which she slid in the pocket of her dress. She buried the other papers, then jumped up and sauntered over to the concession stand.

I waded deeper into the water. Keeping my balance as I walked across the pebbles was tricky. It required my full attention. I reached out to catch a school of light green minnows, but they slipped through my fingers. Then Mother called out, "Do you want some melon?"

"No thank you," I said.

"Go find Lea and see if she does," Mother said. I crossed the beach, retracing Lea's footsteps in the sand, trying to place my foot exactly where her foot had tread. I found her talking with the young man who had told us we couldn't sit beneath the umbrellas. In one ear he wore a strange blue earring in the shape of a Z. He was smoking while Lea stood with one hand on her hip, chatting in Italian.

I thought she looked very grown-up. When she took a puff of his cigarette, I could not believe her audacity.

I kept glancing back at my parents, wondering if they saw what I saw. Then Lea gestured for me to come over. I ran over. She slipped her hand into her pocket then passed me a note. "Give it to Prue. It's a secret. Don't let anyone see." The young Italian teased Lea about her *innamorati*.

Upon reaching the grown-ups, however, I heard Mother say, "Really, I don't believe we should be having this conversation."

"Why not," Prue said.

"I don't know," Mother said. "I just don't."

"But why?" Prue said.

"I'm sorry," Mother said.

"Why do you always say you're sorry?" Prue said.

"What do you want me to say?" Mother said.

"Oh God!" Prue said.

"Very well, I'm not sorry," Mother said.

"Now, now," Father said.

"Oh be quiet," Mother said.

"So you do still have a temper," Prue said.

"Of course I do," Mother said.

At this point, Father interjected, "What on earth are you talking about?"

"Nothing," Mother said and looked down at her hands.

"Where is Lea?" Father suddenly asked.

He turned to me. I pointed in the direction of the umbrella where Lea and the young Italian no longer stood. Father seemed satisfied anyway with the explanation and lay back on his chaise longue.

Mother asked if I wanted to go swimming. I agreed, knowing that this was just an excuse to get away from the others. I would give the note to Prue as soon as I returned. Now was clearly not the right moment. I hid the note inside one of my red sneakers.

Mother held her neck straining upwards so that her hair did not get wet. We swam quite far, to where the sea was very deep and the waters black. You could not see your feet. That was another anomaly of the Cervo beach. It started off very shallow but then suddenly the floor dropped.

When I returned to the beach, there was still no sign of Lea. Mr. Ashton was giving Prue a back massage. I remember staring at his hands, noticing that there was nothing that distinguished his hands from anyone else's. They were quite ordinary, neither big nor small, neither particularly hairy nor smooth, the nails clean and cut neatly. Their very ordinariness was frightening. I lay down on the sand and played a game. I closed my eyes, counted to ten, then opened my eyes to see if Lea had returned. I noticed the young man with the blue earring strutting over to a family of seven who had just sat down beneath the hotel's umbrellas.

I kept waiting for the right moment to give Prue the note. Prue and Mr. Ashton sat side by side and I could not see how to give her the note without his noticing. I also didn't want to have to walk so close to him, imagined that he might reach out and grab me by the ankle, though I knew this was unlikely in front of the other grown-ups. As time passed, the task seemed more difficult. Hungry after the long walk and swim, we all ate voraciously. It was already late, around two-thirty. Melon juice dripped down Mr. Ashton's chin onto the hair of his chest. Prue picked up the entire carcass of the chicken to gnaw it. Father kept pouring everyone more wine. Mother looked flushed from the wine or the sun or both. Even I stuffed myself, with Pecorino, a specialty of the island I particularly liked: goat cheese that was oddly shaped, like a pear, wrapped in pale yellow wax and tied at the top by a string.

We ate in silence. I have no doubt that this reinforces my impression of gluttony. No one commented on Lea's prolonged absence. I myself was not alarmed.

Soon the grown-ups slept. Father slept with his book resting on his chest, his hat covering his face, Mother with her head resting on one arm. Mr. Ashton's mouth was wide open and drool dripped down one side of his face. As for Prue, wasps kept hovering around her hands, drawn to the grease that still glistened on her fingers.

Time dragged by and still I had not accomplished my mission. I decided to look for Lea. I plodded to the back of the beach. This caused me some anxiety. Even though I knew Mr. Ashton was sleeping, I could not bear the thought of losing sight of the others. I kept looking back toward the beach. From time to time, I would reach inside my pocket and feel Lea's note. I peered inside the dark changing cabins, but didn't venture inside. As I peered into the last one, I saw Lea's hat, hanging from one wall. I raced in as fast as I could, breathing fast. The floor seemed cold and I did not like the feel of the damp dust that clung to my toes. I grabbed Lea's white hat, raced out as fast as I could.

I decided to give the note to Prue even if I had to awaken her, but when I saw her sleeping, her face buried in her husband's chest, I could not.

It was then I read the note. She had written it with her best penmanship, the elegant archaic letters we were taught in school. "Dear Prue, Meet me in Mr. Petrinelli's garden by the wall at three-thirty. Love, Lea."

The grown-ups continued to sleep. They hardly changed positions, Prue's face still buried in Mr. Ashton's chest. Father lay on his back with his feet sticking over the end of the chair, Mother on the chair beside him. Now and then she brushed her cheek as if she felt a fly.

Glancing at Father's watch, I saw that it was already three. There was no time to lose.

I slid Lea's note into Prue's straw basket. I considered waking Prue to ensure that she would get the note in time but I did not have the courage.

Keeping Mother and Father in sight, I roamed in and out of coves, over rocks, some of which were smooth, others abrasive. I stopped to stare at crabs in pools of warm water. I did not like standing in the pools because of the damp moss and seaweed. The warm water felt unclean. On and on I rambled. At last, realizing that I had walked much farther than I had intended, I tried to take a shortcut through the dried bushes instead of returning along the rocky coves. I followed a narrow path that suddenly ended. I tried to push my way through the bushes but it was too difficult. There were many other paths once used by hunters or shepherds, but they too ended abruptly, or meandered, ending up back at their point of departure.

By the time I reached the Cervo beach, the sun was no longer at its zenith and I could feel the onset of evening. The sky was turning pink, casting a shadow across the sea. The tops of the trees were gold.

The grown-ups were awake.

"Lea," Father called out, mistaking me because I wore her hat. He seemed disappointed when I turned. He asked where she was.

"I don't know," I said.

He tapped Mother's shoulder with his book.

"Lea is still not back," he said.

"I'm always telling her not to wander off too far. But she

doesn't listen. Do you remember that time we were at Chenon-ceaux and she disappeared for several hours on a tour of the dungeons?"

"What about you? Did you see Lea?" Father asked, turning to the Ashtons.

"No," Mr. Ashton said.

"Which way did you go?" he asked.

"Just a little ways up the hill," Mr. Ashton said.

I felt faint at the thought that I might have met him on my walk.

"Perhaps she's gone over to the Piccolo Pevero," Prue suggested.

The grown-ups were not seriously alarmed. They expected her to show up any minute. Father said he would walk over to the Piccolo Pevero. I offered to go with him. Ascending the steep hill, I had trouble keeping up with him. He was tall and had very long legs. As we climbed, he told me about how he had gotten lost once as a child with his mother in a department store. How he had stopped to look at a toy train and when he turned she had disappeared.

I felt out of breath, as if there were not enough oxygen.

There were fewer people at the Piccolo Pevero beach, but it was still crowded. Families were packing up their bags, folding their umbrellas. I caught sight of a girl swimming far out at sea. "There," I said to Father, pointing to the girl, but as she drew closer to the shore I realized that it was an older woman in her fifties.

I dropped back a few feet when Father walked with the white

hat from one group of people to the next, describing Lea and asking if they had seen her. She's about this tall. He put out one hand to indicate her height. Then he made a gesture to describe her long hair. One person said that they thought they had seen her, several hours earlier. "Sì, sì," they said. "She was standing over there, and then she went off in that direction." Another couple said they thought they had seen her go in the opposite direction. An older woman told Father that he should keep a closer eye on his children and Father got angry. "It's none of your fucking business," he said.

By the time we left the Piccolo Pevero, Father was red in the face. He held my hand and we raced up the hill along the path, back to the Cervo beach, where we found the others sitting silently staring at the sea.

"She's not there," Father said.

"I wonder where she could be?" Mother said.

"Perhaps she's gone home," I suggested.

No one talked as we hurried back up the hill and then down past the turquoise water of the Piccolo Pevero, across the soft white sand. Passing the golf course, I noticed for the first time that you could hear the sound of the water as it fell from the fountains into the small ponds.

I expected to see Lea standing beneath the arch that one passed under before reaching the villa. I imagined it so clearly that I can still picture her in her white dress, an oleander provocatively stuck behind her ear. But there was no one. The house was silent.

Still the grown-ups did not say anything.

I ran out into the garden, past the lemon tree heavy with

lemons, the brilliant red hibiscus, the plumbago. I climbed Mr. Petrinelli's wall. Everything was still. I kept staring at the pine trees, imagining that she would emerge from them.

Then Mother called and I ran back to the house, expecting to see Lea. But when I reached the living room, she was not there. Mother had changed into a navy blue dress with a white belt. Prue was smoking. Mr. Ashton was still taking his shower. "I think we should call the police," Father said.

"Oh, no, really," Mother said. "Lea has done this on several occasions. Once she disappeared with Helen until midnight. Do you remember that, darling?"

"Yes," I said, looking down at my feet.

"I still think we should call the police," Father said.

"I'm sure she'll be back any minute," Mother said, smoothing with one hand the slip on the armrest of her armchair.

"What if she's been kidnapped?" Father said.

"Oh no," Mother said. "Why on earth—Lea?"

"I know, it's not as if we are—" Father said, "mere paupers next to most of the people here."

"Maybe—" I started to say. "I think, hum—"

"What?" Father said.

"Nothing," I said.

"Perhaps we should call Adriana," Mother said. "Perhaps she's gone to visit her."

"She hasn't done that in a long time," Father said.

They tried to call Adriana's home, but the phone was out of order.

In the end, Father prevailed. We would drive to the police

station. The Ashtons suggested they stay at the villa. I insisted on going with Mother and Father.

Father drove the Jeep very fast. If Mother had not reminded him of the gate, he would have driven right through it. He drove at top speed down the hill. We almost hit a car coming round a corner. I knocked my head on the roof as we went over a bump.

Of the police station, I recall the shadow of the fan, one blade magnified in the corner of the room, the flickering photographs in white and black of wanted men, mostly from the Red Brigade, the bars on the small square window, the carabiniere who slowly punched in the information with two fingers, the room feeling smaller and smaller as more carabinieri gathered. One man kept staring at himself in the glass frame of a poster.

Mother and Father argued. They could not agree on the clothes Lea was wearing. They could not agree on the time she had disappeared. Mother said noon. Father thought it was closer to two. They had a long discussion about whether Lea had disappeared before or after Mother had taken her swim, even though neither of them knew at what time she had done that. The carabinieri wanted to know why we had waited so many hours before reporting Lea's disappearance. Father said that Lea often went off for several hours. They wanted to know what she was wearing, the color of her eyes, her hair, her height, her weight, and date of birth. They wanted to know whom Mother and Father socialized with, who came to our house, whether we had received any threats, whether we had noticed anything unusual. They wanted to know if someone had called for a ransom.

"Not yet," Mother said, "but perhaps it's not a kidnapping. Perhaps she'll be back when we get to the villa. I'm sure she will. She's done this several times before. Why don't we try calling the villa? Maybe the phone's back in order." Mother talked nonstop, reiterating the same thing, that she was sure everything would be fine, until Father slammed his fist on the steel table and said, "Shut up," jolting the typewriter. The carabiniere who typed the information kept apologizing that the chief of police was not there. He was out on a case, *molto importante*. The carabiniere kept repeating *molto importante* until Father said, "This is a fucking *molto importante* case."

I became aware that the electric lights had been switched on and that it was dark outside and I could no longer make sense of the Italian. I stared at the black-and-white photographs. One man had his hair plastered the same way as Mr. Ashton. But he wore a mustache. I started to point at the photograph, but Mother said, "Oh darling, not now. No questions." I lay down on a couch with plastic orange cushions. There was a hole in one cushion and I kept pulling out the yellow sponge, and then pushing it in. "Come on, darling. We're going home now. The police are going to follow us."

In the car, on the way back to the house, the night was very black and the air warm and there were thousands of stars. When we passed a car, Mother's face was illuminated. The bones stood out and she looked almost like somebody else.

"I can't bear it," she said.

"There's nothing we can do," Father said. "Just hope for the best. Maybe someone will have called."

"They don't know what they're doing," Mother said.

"They said they would search the beach, that whole area," he said. "They want to make sure she didn't drown."

"Oh no," Mother said. "It's impossible. The water is completely flat and Lea is a wonderful swimmer."

"I don't know why they want to come to the house," Father said. "What do they expect to find there?"

"Perhaps she will be back," Mother said. "Perhaps all this will just be a bad dream."

I imagined the carabinieri beaming their flashlights. Their dogs. I imagined them encountering a herd of wild boars.

From time to time, I would turn round to see if the police car was still following.

Father drove very fast and as we flew round a particularly sharp curve I wondered if we would go over the rampart as other cars were rumored to have done. The flattened railing had still not been put back into place.

The stone archway leading to our villa stood out against the dark, the slab of granite, where the name of our villa should have been inscribed, still blank, and the flowers, the verbena with its tiny red and orange flowers, the white jasmine, glowed in the reflection of strategically placed electric lights.

Even as a child, I felt the contrast between the garden—the air fragrant with the scent of rosemary and of oleander and of juniper, the air liquid—and Lea's absence.

Prue ran up the path, breathlessly, one hand against her chest, the silver heels of her blue shoes catching the light.

"She hasn't come back," she said. "Two journalists showed up. I sent them off."

"Are you sure they were journalists?" Mother asked. "Could they have been sent by the kidnappers?"

"Hardly," Prue said. "Besides, they showed me their cards." A bulb flashed and we caught sight of a man as he stepped from behind a bush. Father rushed up to him and yelled, "Get the fuck out of here—"

Another journalist appeared on the doorstep. He said that he could help us. He would be happy to write a letter from us to the kidnappers. Front page. Two policemen stepped up. They said something to the journalists, who then waited outside.

The villa soon filled with people—neighbors whom we knew only by sight: the famous piano maker from Germany and his wife, the funeral home director—more and more carabinieri.

The police kept asking Father and Mother the same questions. I stayed close by them, but it was sometimes difficult because there were so many people. At least there was no sign of Mr. Ashton. I was glad when Adriana arrived. She took me by her small firm hand and settled me on her lap, as if I were four or five. She held me tight, repeating, "Poverina, poverina," and I felt as if she were referring not only to Lea but to me.

From where Adriana and I were seated we could see out into the lit garden. Some reporters had climbed the stone wall that surrounded the garden, even trees, and it frightened me to see their dark shapes. They looked like monkeys hanging from branches.

It got later and later. The phone was repaired, but still people stayed.

At last Father exploded, "Why are you staying here? She is not here. Go and find her. Don't you see that we are wasting time? We don't know where she is or we would go and get her. Get out. Leave."

At last we were alone, and Adriana drew the blinds in the living room, locked the windows and doors. Mr. Ashton reappeared. He sat down beside Prue and Father on the sofa while Mother sat in a chair opposite them. I curled up on the white carpet at her feet. We all waited for the phone to ring. Sometimes I imagined that I heard it. It was a cream-colored rotary phone, with a red button that you had to push in order to hear the incoming voice. Without the sound of the wind in the background, the clock seemed loud. I heard it chime every hour. I counted the chimes. Every now and then I thought I heard footsteps, a knock at the door. I kept wondering if Prue had found the note.

I awakened at dawn. A strange blue light filled the living room. The sky was a pale blue streaked with purple. In the distance an island, a darker shade of blue, emerged and then receded. Gradually, the purple streaks turned pink. The sky whitened, becoming a light pink, then reverted to a pale blue. At a quarter past six the sun was up. It was a perfect day with not a breath of wind.

Lea had now been gone approximately thirteen to fifteen hours.

A clock chimed and I turned away from the sky. I found myself staring at Prue's feet. I examined them closely, noticing that an odd bone protruded like a knob from the top of her left foot, another bone from the inside. Her toes were scarred with thin white lines.

Mr. Ashton's legs lay over hers. He had not taken off his leather shoes. He had not even unlaced them.

I slipped my hand inside Prue's straw basket. The note was still there. I wondered when she would find it, whether she would say anything, if she would think that Lea had put it there herself, whether it would have made any difference had she got it.

There was no sign of Mother or Father.

I heard the sound of a shower, a broom brushing across tiles. On the patio outside the kitchen, I found Adriana sweeping bougainvillea. She did not brush them into one pile but from one side of the patio to the other. She was muttering to herself. When she caught sight of me, she stopped.

"I felt something bad was going to happen," she said.

"How?" I asked, feeling sick.

"Here." She touched her chest. She leaned over and pulled some of the purple flowers that had become entangled in the broom. "You better have something to eat. You're going to the police station this morning."

At the mention of food, I felt even more ill.

I ran to the bathroom with Adriana following me. I threw up. I recall staring into the toilet bowl at tiny white pieces of food, finding it impossible to believe that these morsels had once been Pecorino cheese. Adriana wiped my face with a damp washcloth then combed my hair.

13

The villa seemed too quiet. I kept listening for the sound of shutters rattling, or of sand against glass. Hearing a cry, I imagined it was Lea calling for help, but it was just a bird. The silence of the wind amplified other sounds. People's footsteps echoed.

At the police station, voices seemed unnaturally loud. When a carabiniere slapped down magazines on a table, I jumped in my seat. The voice of an American drifted into the room from a hallway I could see from my chair. "I heard that you had to be careful on the island but who would have thought—" The door slammed. Now, of course, I realize that I was probably sensitive to sounds because I had slept only a few hours.

Through the bars of the window I could see the bare branches of a tree. The night before, on our way out of the police station, in the reflection of a street lamp, I had noticed the petals around its base, a pool of pink.

As we waited, Father kept brushing absentmindedly the lapel of his jacket. But there was no dust, not even a pink petal. Mother sat very straight, her back not touching the chair, her knees drawn together, her handbag resting in her lap. She wore a purple pleated skirt with a matching jacket, white sandals, and even stockings. I had not wanted to wear the dress she had chosen for me. I had insisted on wearing a velvet mustard-colored dress with a brown chocolate sash, much too warm for the weather, pink plastic sandals that belonged to Lea. I kept slipping the sandals on and off my feet. Mr. Ashton folded a piece of paper, turning it into a hat, then a boat. The Ashtons still wore their rumpled clothes from the night before.

Another door in the hallway opened and this time I caught a glimpse of Mr. Peters slumped in a chair. His nose was bleeding. He stared in my direction but did not see me. The door closed. I heard footsteps. Another carabiniere appeared to say that the chief of police would be with us momentarily. Father muttered, "Shit," under his breath. He strode over to the window. He drew a breath from his cigarette then crushed it and threw it out.

I slipped my sandals off again. I stared at the door behind which Mr. Peters was concealed. There were so many doors. I counted six on one side of the hallway and seven on the other. Were people in every room? I wondered which door was the bathroom door. I had to go very badly. I twisted my legs twice. I did not want to ask.

The waiting room, which smelled faintly of salami, gradually grew hotter and hotter. A carabiniere came in and turned on the ceiling fan. But it did little to cool us. The heat was stifling. The sun beat mercilessly through the bars of the window. I watched the shadow of the fan as it gradually sank lower, wondering what would happen if the fan dropped.

Suddenly, the chief of police appeared in the doorway. I did not recognize him at once as the man who had stood rubbing cream into his hand during an earlier visit. In his own domain, he projected a very different impression. His age was hard to establish. To me, as a child, of course, he seemed very old, but he was probably in his fifties. He was dressed completely in black and looked more like a priest than a chief of police. He wore his clothes tight. He was bald, short, around five feet six, but compact. Nevertheless, even when he sat, one leg thrown nonchalantly over one side of a chair, he seemed to dwarf everyone, including father, who was a foot taller than he.

I remember Mother later remarking that the chief of police was unusual in that while he asked questions, he also provided information about himself. Mother told me that he had not always been a chief of carabinieri. He had been, amongst other things, a teacher, a dancer, an amateur chef, even an actor, which last she could well believe because he liked to mimic and act out scenes. He came from a family of carpenters.

The chief of police apologized for keeping us waiting. "Unfortunately," he said, "you are not the only kidnapping." He insisted on interviewing us one at a time. Mother went in first. We heard her pleading, "She will be all right? They won't do anything to her. It's all my fault. I know it is. If only—" When she emerged, her hair had slipped out of her bun. Her handbag had opened. She did not say anything as she sat back down on her chair and placed her handbag on her knees.

Father went in next. I heard his muffled sobs. I avoided looking at Mother and the Ashtons. I remembered Lea doing her handstand against the wall, asking whether the man who had been kidnapped would have his ear cut off.

The door opened and I caught sight of the chief of police leaning forward, passing Father a glass of water, sliding a box of tissues across the table. The chief of police said something. Father shook his head. The door closed.

The Ashtons did not speak either. Now and then, Mr. Ashton cleared his throat. He had explained to Lea and me that he had bad respiratory problems. As a boy his mother always knew when the north wind was going to blow because he got a cold. He had spent his childhood in bed.

When Father emerged, his face was streaked with tears. His skin was mottled. He did not sit down but paced the room.

Mother accompanied me into the chief of police's office. She held my hand tightly in hers. I hardly said a word. Each time he asked me a question, Mother answered for me. He insisted on helping Mother out of her jacket, on opening the door for her, even fetching water, coffee. On his desk he kept a box of tissues, which he pushed over. He kept coming back to the last time I had seen Lea.

"Let's start from the very beginning again," the chief of police said, leaning forward in his chair, resting his elbows on his knees, his chin in his hands. He gazed kindly at me. I started to say that Lea had been talking to a young Italian with a blue earring.

"The same who told us that we could not sit under the umbrellas?" Mother interpolated.

"Yes," I said.

The chief of police said, "Continue." I looked down at his

shoes. They were black. Then Mother reached out and placed a strand of hair behind my ear.

He did not push for an elaboration. I wiped my palms on the skirt of my dress. "Have they found the young man?" Mother asked.

"Not yet," he said. "We will, but the island is big. What about Mr. Peters?"

Mother switched to Italian. She talked very fast. She had a very strong English accent and I felt terribly embarrassed, wishing she would speak English, focusing on the nameplate where the chief of police's name was inscribed. Rossi. I read it over and over again.

"And you?" he asked me. "When did you see Mr. Peters?" Mother looked over at me. I remembered Mr. Peters following us. I looked at Mother.

"He followed us," I said.

"This was before or after?" the chief of police asked.

"Before," I said.

The chief of police did not speak for a moment. Mother and I watched as he applied Scotch tape to a tear in a newspaper.

Then he asked about Lea's hat. Where had I found it? I told him that it had been hanging from one of the pegs in the changing room, and he nodded as if that made sense. He wanted to know what Lea's mood had been that day. But again, before I could reply, Mother answered for me. "Oh Lea is always very cheerful, always laughing, always making fun."

"Do you remember anything unusual? Did anything occur in the past few days out of the ordinary?" he asked.

I felt this was directed at me. My mind went blank, then I remembered what had happened with Mr. Ashton in the bathroom. But I felt unable to say anything. It would be too embarrassing. Mother would ask me why I hadn't told anyone before now. And what was the point when there couldn't possibly be any connection between what had happened to me and Lea's disappearance? All I seemed able to focus on was the note, the fact that I had not given it immediately to Prue. But even this I felt I could not confide.

The interview lasted only a few minutes. Mother said, "Is that all? Don't you want to ask more questions?"

"For the moment that will be all," the chief of police said.

Beneath Mr. Ashton's chair, I noticed a small pile of folded hats and boats. Father still stood at the window with his back to us. The chief of police asked Prue to follow him.

Prue spent a long time in Mr. Rossi's office. By now, despite the fan, the heat was unbearable. Mr. Ashton pulled out a handkerchief from his pocket and wiped his forehead. Mother fell asleep for a few minutes in her chair, her head slowly sliding sideways. I kept moving forward in my seat because my dress was sticking to my back. I remembered that I had had to go to the bathroom, but the urge had disappeared.

At last Prue emerged. She placed her hand on Mr. Rossi's shoulder. She smiled, but her smile seemed strained. "Now, I'd like to talk with Mr. Ashton," Mr. Rossi said.

Mother, Father, and I waited out in the courtyard for Mr. Ashton to be done. Although there was still no breeze, it was a relief not to be confined in the small room. We stood beneath the tree. Father smoked while Mother stood hugging herself. She complained that she was cold despite the heat. I collected tiny pink petals that surrounded the tree, cradling them in my hands then letting them drop, over and over again, until Mr. and Mrs. Ashton appeared, with Prue leaning on Mr. Ashton as if she had trouble walking on her own.

On the way back, as the Jeep skirted the azure sea, sped past white villas reflecting the sunlight, purple bougainvillea blazing, sprinklers shooting water across the green lawns, the grown-ups discussed the chief of police. Father kept referring to him as the annoying bastard or the supercilious bastard. "The bastard said how unusual it was for children to be allowed to wander off for hours on their own. I suppose I'm of the old school. Self-satisfied bastard," Father said. "Never says anything directly, of course, it's just in the tone, the way he repeats what you say. 'So she was gone several hours?' That sort of thing."

Mother said she didn't think he was that bad. Yes, he was annoying at times, but he was understanding, accommodating.

"Accommodating!" Father exclaimed. "He's an ass."

"All right, darling," Mother said. "Do concentrate on the road."

Prue said he was all right but his pants were too tight. Mr. Ashton said he could not judge but that he fancied there was more to the man than met the eye.

"He is always a step ahead of you," Mother said.

"If you ask me, they're a bunch of incompetent fools," Father said. "Instead of interviewing us they should be interviewing the real suspects."

"Like the young Italian man Lea was talking to," Mother interjected.

"What young man?" Father asked.

"The one who told us we could not sit beneath the umbrella," Mother said. "Helen saw them."

"What did you see?" Father asked.

"They walked to the cabin," I said.

"So they went back to the cabin," Mr. Ashton said, rubbing his unshaven chin.

"I wonder—" Mother started to say.

"The chief of police wouldn't tell me if he had interviewed or even found the young man," Prue said.

"Oh so you knew about him too," Father said. "It seems as if—"

"I didn't see him either," Mr. Ashton said.

This was the only time they addressed me. For the remainder of the drive they referred to me in the third person, as if I were not present. At the time I did not mind. I wanted only to think of Lea.

"What about Helen, what did they ask her?" Father asked Mother.

"Not much," Mother said.

"She never does say much," Father said.

I stared at the branches of the trees reflected in the car window. They made me think of the sea, the sea urchins we had found at the beginning of the summer. I pictured the fragmented light on the white sand, the dark areas I had ventured into with Lea. I was lying in the back of the Jeep on the floor. It was hot but I liked the smell of the rubber mat in the sun. I felt a sudden release, something warm flow down my leg, and realized I had peed.

"What do you suppose Mr. Peters was doing at the station?" I heard Mrs. Ashton say.

"I hope they're not wasting their time on him," Father said.

"Perhaps he was there for something unrelated," Mother said.

"Really?" Prue said. "Like what?"

"I don't know," Mother said.

"Bound to be an islander," Mr. Ashton said. "Almost always is in these cases."

"If she has been kidnapped," Mother said.

"Where do you think she is?" Father asked. "On some kind of fucking vacation?"

"Nobody has called for a ransom," Mother said.

"That is odd," Prue said.

"There is still time," Mr. Ashton said.

"Oh I can't bear it," Mother said. "It's all my fault—"

"Yes, that's right. It is all your fault," Father said.

In the rearview mirror I caught sight of Mother hiding her face in her hands.

"Why do you have to do this with everything?" Father asked.

"No, no," Mother said. "We should have paid more attention."

"Yes, we should have, but what good is it to go on and on about it?"

At the villa we all stopped in the entryway and peered into the kitchen. By then my underwear and the skirt of my dress felt cold and clung to my legs. Adriana spoke with her back to us, her arms covered with flour. As she stretched her arms out to knead the dough, her shirt tightened across her back. She complained that the phone had been ringing all morning, nothing from the kidnappers. Several journalists waited in the living room.

Whenever I tried to imagine the kidnappers, my mind went blank. I kept focusing on the note instead. I kept wishing I had given it to Prue sooner.

"I'm going to take the Jeep, drive out into the countryside," Father said turning back round.

"Do be careful," Mother said.

I later found out that Father visited scores of empty houses. Sometimes in the company of a carabiniere but more often on his own.

"I must do something," Mother said. "I must." She too did not feel like speaking with the journalists.

Adriana suggested showing Mother how to roll gnocchi.

"See," Adriana said, twisting a piece of dough with one deft movement of her fingers. Mother tried but hers looked like a little lump of dough.

"You just need practice," Adriana said, continuing.

Mother asked her to slow down. She showed Mother again.

This time Mother's gnocchi approximated the real thing.

"What happened to you?" Adriana asked, noticing my wet clothes.

"I peed in my pants," I said.

"Come with me," she said. "I'll run you a hot bath if there's any water."

"I'll do it," Mother said.

"Good," Adriana said.

I followed Mother down the corridor, begged her to stay with me.

"Of course, my sweet," she said, sitting on the side of the tub, and for a brief moment it was almost as it had been before that summer.

When the chief of police arrived, accompanied by a carabiniere who stammered, he took his time wiping the soles of his black shoes across the straw mat. In one hand, he carried a burgundy briefcase. I heard him say, "Very interesting," an expression I later learned to be a favorite of his. I do not know what he was referring to. Perhaps he was simply noticing the glass jar with the faded sea urchins.

"Have you found out anything?" Mother asked.

Mr. Rossi placed his hand on Mother's shoulder but did not answer her question until the journalists had been dispatched and everyone had gathered around the dining room table and he had replaced his dark glasses for clear ones. "We've located the young man Lea was talking to," he said. "It turns out that he has a record of petty offenses. He's been caught stealing someone's motorcycle, cash from a register. The nephew of the third cousin of Mrs. Martini. I believe you know her?" he turned to Prue.

"Me?" Prue asked, placing her hand on her chest.

"She lives on via Medici," he said. "She does—"

"Ah, yes, the waxing lady," Prue said.

"Do you think," Mother said.

"No, petty vandalism hardly qualifies," the chief of police said. "Why, your own girls—"

"What do you mean?" Father asked, leaning forward.

It was then the chief of police revealed that we were suspected of having burned Mr. Peters's painting. After all that had happened, I had forgotten about it.

I stared down at the table. I ran my fingers along the rough edge. At the time, I was impressed by the rapidity with which he had gathered this information. In fact, the information must have been rather easy to collect.

"They're children," Father said.

"He's only sixteen," the chief of police said. "What about Mr. Peters?"

"I cannot see Mr. Peters kidnapping Lea," Father said.

"What do you think?" the chief of police asked Prue.

"It's entirely possible," Prue said. "He hasn't been quite in his right mind lately." Mr. Rossi did not ask her to elaborate.

"And he drinks," Mr. Ashton said.

"A drinking problem hardly qualifies," Father said. "This is ridiculous. A complete waste of time."

"Quite right," Mr. Ashton said. "We all know it's bound to be an islander. I mean it always is."

"It does make the most sense," Mother said. "If only they would call for a ransom."

"I have to agree," Prue said.

"We will see," the chief of police said. He rubbed his hands.

"Well, what now?" Father asked.

Mr. Rossi had pulled out an envelope from his briefcase. He

applied a piece of Scotch tape across the tear. We all watched him.

"Do you have to do that here?" Father asked.

"You have my complete attention," the chief of police said.

"Let me see," Prue said. "Who can we think of? At the hotel where we had dinner once, Lea talked for a long time with the pizza man who baked pizzas in the shape of her name, I mean initial, you might—"

"This is all very interesting," Mr. Rossi said.

"We don't find it interesting," Father said. He covered his face with his hands and I thought he would cry. Mr. Rossi placed his hand on Father's back, then stood up. He asked if we had received any mail. Just two letters but nothing from the kidnappers. He said they must look through Lea's effects.

It was strange to see men fingering Lea's clothes. The carabiniere looked over everything. Finding a stray hair on one collar, he placed it within a small plastic bag. He discovered a notebook of mine from the summer before. In it, Lea and I had written all the things we wanted to do in the future. She wanted to be an actress and visit our great-aunt the pianist in Saint Petersburg. I wanted to live in the country with four cats and dogs and write books. "We used to play a game," I said. The chief of police placed his hand on my shoulder as if to steady me.

I felt his gaze upon me.

They discovered objects long forgotten: an old toy lamb, a box filled with shells, a sheet of paper where Lea had written columns with the names of flowers, capitals, countries. Most disturbing was a new secret cache beneath her mattress I had no knowledge of, objects I had never seen before: a single pink kid glove that fastened at the elbow with three pearls, a gold cuff link with the initials J.A., and an exquisite green Buddha.

Here was the proof I had suspected all along: a whole side of Lea that she had been hiding.

That afternoon I started to haunt Prue. She could go nowhere without me trailing behind. Several times I frightened her. Once while she was bathing. A trellis covered the glass window outside her bathroom. I pushed back the leaves and peered inside. She dropped the soap. Perhaps she imagined for a moment that I was Lea. A little later, as she rambled down the path of the garden, I watched her from my perch on top of the wall. She seemed to be searching for something. She peered behind bushes, along the wall. I imagined that she was seeking some evidence, but it turned out to be nothing more ominous than the hose.

14

The second day the islands were the exact color of the sky, the only sound a mosquito buzzing. The sun beat down on the tiled roof of the villa. I imagined a monster leaning over, breathing hot air into our house. Looking back, I have an impression of darkness too, broken only by thin threads of light, because Adriana had closed the heavy wood shutters. But this seemed to have only trapped the heat further. The floors were no longer cool. There was nowhere to find relief, except in the sea, but, of course, we couldn't think of swimming with Lea still missing. For days we had been imprisoned by the wind, now it was the sun. We waited for the chief of police. He had called to say that he was going to be late. We decided that he was on to something.

I can see Prue slapping a mosquito on her arm. She said she almost wished for the wind to return. She was wearing a purple skirt and a simple cotton shirt with pearl buttons. I noted that the tiny pearl buttons were not real but constructed of white plastic baubles covered with silver paper. I observed the way she reached back, letting out the waist of her skirt.

"Why are you staring at me like that?" she asked.

"I'm sorry," I muttered, looking down.

She sent me to get another of the green coils we used to keep the mosquitoes away. They gave off a strange odor but only half worked.

"Have you ever seen so many bites?" Prue asked Father when he returned from town with the local newspaper. Father spread it across the dining room table. I ran over. Someone opened a shutter halfway to let in some light. Mother emerged from her room. We all stood around Father. The headlines on the front page ran something like this: ANOTHER KIDNAPPING? THIRTEEN-YEAR-OLD AMERICAN GIRL DISAPPEARS MYSTERIOUSLY AT THE CERVO BEACH. At first, I did not connect it with Lea. We had lived in France so long I did not think of us as Americans. But then I saw her photograph. She stared out at me, laughing. I remembered how she had made me braid her hair again and again until the parting was dead straight and not one hair was out of place. I had tied large navy blue bows at the end of each braid. She looked very young in the photograph. It was hard to believe the picture had been taken only a few weeks before.

The article talked very little about the actual kidnapping. I suppose there was not much information to go on. It dwelled mostly on the escalation of the number of kidnappings. How this would affect tourism. People were actually safer on the island than on the mainland, the writer insisted. It was a grave mistake to conclude that all the kidnappings were done by islanders. More often than not kidnappers were imported from the mainland. One should not jump to any conclusions, particularly in this case, when no ransom had been requested. I garnered this information because Prue did not understand Italian and she asked Mother to translate.

By the time the chief of police arrived, dressed in khaki pants this time, wearing sunglasses, which he carefully folded and placed inside a black case, everyone was on edge. When he did not announce any news, but simply apologized for the delay, Father lost his temper. Father told him that the investigation was getting nowhere. What had they found? Perhaps he should hire a private detective.

The chief of police replied in a measured tone. Nothing seemed to fluster him.

"That is entirely up to you," he said. "We are doing our best." They had talked to the pizza man Prue had mentioned, a most unlikely candidate. He had been working a double shift at the hotel. The cabdriver had been with his wife and daughter.

"Well," Father said. "Have you discovered anything? Do you have any leads?"

"We spoke to your neighbor, Mr. Petrinelli. He says that he saw Lea walking through the garden around four."

"What was she doing there?" Mother asked. "Where did she go? Who's Mr. Petrinelli?"

"The man who asked me to cut down our pine trees because they are blocking his view of the sea," Father said.

"Could he—"

The chief of police turned to me, but at this point, Adriana stepped out from the kitchen. "Scusi," she said. She asked if she could talk to Mr. Rossi for a moment. She held one hand in the pocket of her dress. Mr. Rossi followed her into the kitchen. We overheard Adriana speak excitedly in the dialect of the island.

When the chief of police emerged, he said that he would like to speak to Prue.

We watched the chief of police and Prue step out into the sun onto the patio. The chief of police said something. Prue shook her head. He reached into his pocket, then pulled his hand out and opened his palm. Pieces of paper drifted to the ground. He leaned over to gather them. The chief of police asked Prue something else and Prue went into a long explanation, waving her arms dramatically in the air, touching the chief of police's cuff now and then. The chief of police nodded. I thought I heard her say, "No." At one point, she turned and seemed to point at me.

"What do you suppose all that's about?" Father asked.

"She seems very upset," Mother said.

"So sensitive," said Mr. Ashton, who had emerged from his room.

Mother and Father glanced at one another. This adjective couldn't have been more inappropriate to describe Mrs. Ashton.

When Prue returned to the table, we all pretended not to have watched. I looked down and brushed crumbs into the embroidered seams of the tablecloth.

Prue took a long time to readjust her skirt before sitting down.

"I would like to talk to Helen," Mr. Rossi said.

"To Helen?" Mother said.

"Really?" Father asked.

I stood up. I felt everyone watch me as I walked across the room. I was about to step out onto the patio when I heard Prue say, "You had no right to go through my wastepaper basket." Mr. Rossi turned back.

Prue now stood facing Adriana, who had just emerged from the kitchen.

"I only did what I thought was best," Adriana said.

"Right," Prue said, muttering something under her breath.

"I don't understand what you say," Adriana said. "But I won't be talked to like that."

Mr. Ashton got up and placed his arm around Prue's shoulders. "Please excuse her. She is very upset." He pulled her away.

"We are all very upset," Adriana said, rolling up her apron.

"Yes," Mother said.

"Right," Father said.

Mr. Rossi stepped outside. I followed, shading my eyes immediately with one hand. The glare of the sun was so strong that all the different flowers seemed to fade into one kind. It was hard to breathe.

The sun glanced off Mr. Rossi's bald head. He walked slowly, with his hands clasped behind his back. I focused on the way his shadow passed through the shadows of trees. I dragged my feet to ensure that Lea's pink plastic sandals did not fall off. I kept glancing back at the villa, the purple bougainvillea cascading across the roof.

Suddenly, he stopped in the shade of a tree. "Mr. Petrinelli says that he saw Lea walking through his garden with someone."

"Not me," I said at last. "Maybe he saw her with Carla or Prue."

"Who's Carla?" Mr. Rossi asked.

"Adriana's niece," I said.

"Why Mrs. Ashton?"

"I don't know," I said. "They had a fight."

"A fight?" he said.

I exaggerated and said that I had seen Prue push Lea across the deck. Lea had almost fallen into the sea, I said.

I felt that if Prue had not rejected Lea so cruelly, she would not have tried to arrange a meeting, intended, I was sure, to reconcile.

"What about this note?" Mr. Rossi said.

"Lea gave it to me to give to Prue," I said. "I put it in her bag, but very late and she didn't see it."

Then Mr. Rossi asked me why Lea had burned Mr. Peters's painting.

"I don't know," I said.

"Did she not like Mr. Peters?" he asked.

"In the beginning she did," I said.

"In the beginning?" he asked.

"Before Prue," I said.

"What happened?" he said.

"I don't know," I said, picturing Mother and Mr. Peters lying on the couch.

"Did Lea like the Ashtons?" he asked.

"Oh yes," I said. "Prue especially, but then they got into a fight and—at the picnic, she wanted—but she did not like Mr. Ashton."

"Oh," he said, "and why is that?"

"She said he was a bore and to the right of Genghis Khan," I said.

He placed his hand on my shoulder and we ascended the path to the shaded veranda. He pointed to one of the yellow-and-white fold-out chairs. I sat down. He went inside the villa and came back out with his burgundy briefcase, which he balanced across his knees. He drew vertical then horizontal lines through his notebook. I thought I saw one of the grown-ups peer through the glass door, but because of the reflection of the sun off the glass, all I could see was the shadow of a face.

"Did you see Lea talk to anyone else besides the young man at the beach?" he asked.

"No," I said, glad to be able to tell the truth.

From his briefcase he pulled black-and-white photographs. "Tell me if you recognize anyone," he said.

I stared diligently at each photograph.

"You can go now," he said. "I will speak with Mr. Ashton."

A few moments later, I joined Mother, Father, and Prue, who were still sitting around the dining room table. We watched Mr. Ashton take the seat I had just vacated on the patio. He said something, pulled out a cigar and lit it, while Mr. Rossi continued to draw lines in his notebook. Then Mr. Rossi asked Mr. Ashton something and he answered, putting out his cigar hurriedly, without having finished it. Mr. Rossi shook his head and got up. Mr. Ashton followed him.

We all pretended not to notice them crossing the living room but as soon as they stepped out of the villa, we went to the kitchen and watched Mr. Ashton get into Mr. Rossi's car. I saw Adriana knock on the passenger window, then say something. "I wonder what else she's going to make up," Prue remarked.

"I wonder why Mr. Rossi wants to interview him?" Father said.

"Yes," Mother said. "I wonder."

"I can't imagine," Prue said, leaving the kitchen.

I followed her down the shadowy corridor. I expected her to close the door to her bedroom but she left it ajar. When I peered in, she was sitting in front of the mirror in her room, her face hidden in her hands. She uttered a terrible moan that startled me. In my fright, I opened the door wider, catching sight of my reflection in her mirror as she took her hands from her face. "Go away, go away," she cried.

I raced back down the corridor to my room, hid in Lea's bed. I thought the sheets still smelled of her. I wrapped myself up as tightly as I could.

A little later Mother, Father, and Prue were summoned to the police station. I spent a long time sitting at one of the built-in tables in one of the guest rooms, staring out a window at a wall, watching the progression of a yellow snail gliding along the glass pane. I wondered how it found its way, whether it just glided along until it bumped into something or whether its antennae directed it. Above the small wall orange and yellow flowers grew. A fluorescent lizard slithered over rocks and disappeared.

I felt a hand on my shoulder, turned to see Adriana, who drew me away from the window. She led me to the kitchen, where she had prepared a large bowl of spaghetti with tomatoes and basil. She sat down, rested one elbow on the table and, watching me eat, told me a story I had never heard before. On May 26 in the year 1208, she said, the Madonna appeared to a man who could not speak. "Go and get the other villagers," the Madonna said. Back at the village the man opened his mouth to tell the villagers about the Madonna and found that he was able to talk. The villagers rushed to the beach, where they discovered the statue of the Virgin and child. They placed it in the village's church, but the very next day the statue disappeared, leaving in its place only the branch of an olive tree. They searched all day, all night, until at last one of the villagers spotted the statue in an olive tree, but now carrying the sign, NOLI ME TOLLERE—Do not take me away. The villagers built a church around the Madonna with child.

I asked Adriana to tell me another miracle story, but the telephone rang. I pattered through the villa, which had grown even hotter over the last few hours; the flowers Adriana had placed in vases were drooping, the petals falling one by one. At least my movements were unconfined with the Ashtons at the police station. I found myself drawn to their room.

Apart from a thread of light that cut across their pink bedspread, the room was in the dark. The blue pillbox Lea had stolen now stood among the other pillboxes on top of the chest of drawers. The emerald box too. Everything was covered with the fine ocher dust and even sand had filtered in, glinting in the corners of the room by the sliding door. I opened a drawer, touched with one finger Prue's silk underwear, permeated by her heavy perfume, which reminded me of the scent of old ladies. I found the photograph of the dogs Lea had mentioned. They did look like pigs. They were arranged in a row in front of a pool and they each had different colored collars. I wondered which dog had drowned.

Carefully, I replaced the photograph and closed the drawer, opened another and discovered Mr. Ashton's socks. Unlike Father's socks, which were rolled one sock inside the other, these had been curled by pairs into concentric circles, in a manner that I had never seen before or since. Something glinted from within the center of one pair. I pulled it out—Lea's gold wrist-watch. I dropped it as soon as I realized what it was. I slammed the drawer closed and raced out the room.

I ran down the corridor to my bedroom, where Adriana now sat reading her Bible. "There you are," she said. She had opened the heavy wood blind, surrendering no doubt to the inevitability of the heat. I lay at her feet and watched the sun slowly glide across the tiled floor.

I kept visualising the gold watch in the curled-up sock.

I did not hear the grown-ups come down the corridor. Prue's voice startled me. "He probably already knew."

"But it's got nothing to do with the investigation," Mother said.

"Everyone knows," Prue said.

I thought they had not noticed us so I stood up and said, "Hello," in a loud voice. But that didn't seem to deter them.

"I don't see why—" Mother said.

Adriana closed her Bible and reached for my hand. She asked if I would like to play a game of *scala quaranta* but I did not, then she suggested we go for a *passeggiata* through the garden. It was too hot. I sat down on my bed and she sat down beside me. Her feet, like mine, did not touch the floor.

"We've gone over this before," Prue said.

"But why did you feel obliged to talk about it?" Mother asked.

"What difference does it make?" Prue said.

"To me it does. To me it does," Mother said.

"If anything, I would have thought you would be pleased. Now he's off the hook. Before that it appeared that he was obsessed with Lea. Besides, I'm sure he told the chief of police himself. He's not exactly discreet—"

I understood that they were talking about Mr. Peters and Mother.

Adriana pointed to a stray marmalade cat outside the window of my room. I had never seen it before. She told me that she once owned a cat before she married. "His name was Mimi," she said. She had called him that not knowing that he was male. When she realized that he was male, it was too late. The name had stuck. She told me how she had found him by the garbage cans. How he was all white except for his black paws. But what was most unusual about him was that he did not mind being on a leash, just like a dog, she said. Every evening she took him for his *passeggiata*. Everyone knew her and her white cat. She told me that she had to leave early that day because of a cousin's engagement party.

I remember running along the pathway, the tiles hot like irons beneath my feet, stepping from beneath the archway, in order to catch a last glimpse of her car as she turned the corner. I stood despite the sun bearing down, the top of my head burning. I stared at the low bushes shimmering in the heat, breathed the scent of earth and rocks, until my eyes could no longer stand the glare.

At the villa I found Father standing in the living room by the window. He looked out at the garden. But I sensed by the way he stood, his gaze abstracted, that he did not see the garden. I walked over to him but he stared down at me as if surprised that I existed. Mother sat on the sofa. I placed my hand on her back and she reached for my hand and kissed it but then hurried out of the room. I lay on my stomach across the glass coffee table. Because it had wheels, you could inch across the living room floor. I peered through the glass at the red tiles. I counted fifty-two from one end to the other.

15

The next day was even hotter. Adriana, who arrived punctually at a quarter to ten, said she could not remember the island ever being this hot. "Un inferno," she said and suggested we go for a walk while the grown-ups went to the police station. The Ashtons had not appeared that morning for breakfast and I was glad because I hated eating with Mr. Ashton, having to watch him spoon out the pulp from his fresh orange juice, placing it on a saucer where it drew flies. Sometimes, his mouth would stay half open and I would see his tongue. Mother had said something about Mr. Ashton being questioned for many hours at the police station. Father remarked that he wished he knew what it was all about. He had asked Mrs. Ashton but she seemed to know as little as they did.

On our walk, Adriana and I traveled a different path. Instead of going down toward the beach, we went up, along a ridge where I had never ventured before. She held my hand in hers. I could see the heat rising in waves from bushes that seemed about to burst into flames. Everything was so still it felt difficult to breathe. Adriana told me about her life. During the war, she and her mother and brother had moved from the city to the country. She told me about the planes that flew overhead, how she had hidden behind a bush with her brother, Juan Carlo, and her mother. She told me that her favorite toy was a female Pinocchio whose dress had got ruined in the rain. She traversed a river by stepping across boats that were placed head to toe across the water. They looked like nuns, she said, perhaps because they were painted black-and-white. She had wanted to be a violinist but her parents had no money so she had become a cook at sixteen.

The shadow of a tree I took for Lea's shadow. I stopped. "What is it?" she asked.

"Nothing," I said.

At the beach I saw a girl with blond hair. My heart started to beat faster, but when she turned round, she looked nothing like Lea.

I refused to go swimming, so we sat in the shade watching other people swim, lie beneath their umbrellas, rub on cream, read, laugh, talk.

Adriana attempted to distract me by telling me about the gold pendants that hung from a gold chain around her neck. She explained that she had had the pendants glued to her grandmother's ring, which was too large for her. One was a Saint Christopher, the saint of travelers, the other of Jesus and Mary.

I did not want to leave the beach. I dragged my feet up the hill. I grew quiet as we approached the villa. Adriana had to visit an ailing relative the next day, but she promised to come the day after.

As I drifted round the patio outside the kitchen, picking up the heads of the hibiscus, placing them in the skirt of my dress, I pretended that the flowers were nuns and that each one had a name: Sister Magdalene and Sister Sophie and Sister Claire. I arranged them across the tiles. A strict nun supervised them.

I was so absorbed in my game that I did not hear the grown-ups enter the kitchen.

I heard Mother say, "I just—"

"But—" Prue said.

"Mr. Rossi wanted to know—" Mother said. She sounded frightened but Prue sounded angry.

"If you think—" Prue said.

"I don't know what to think anymore," Mother said. "I just want her back." She stared through the window. She did not see me sitting on the floor of the patio.

"Helen," she called. I was pleased to detect a hint of concern in her voice. "I'm here," I said, running inside the kitchen. Mother suggested we have high tea. Mother and I were the only ones in the family who liked boiled eggs. We cut toast into thin strips that Mother let me dip into the yolk. She told me a story, something she had not done in a long time, about a princess who turned down her suitors. I climbed onto her lap and passed my fingers through her hair.

In the evening, the grown-ups kept fighting. At first it was over insignificant things. The Ashtons had forgotten to turn off the outdoor lights. "Of course, they are not paying for them," Father said. Mother said that the least the Ashtons could have done was buy a bottle of wine or several boxes of spaghetti, instead of just one box for that evening.

"What do you expect?" Father asked.

"Nothing," Mother said.

"They're your friends," he said.

"You invited them," she said.

And as usual the Ashtons were late for dinner.

When Prue sat down, she apologized for their tardiness.

Father shrugged then served himself a large plate of spaghetti. Mother served Prue and Mr. Ashton.

I pretended to feed my doll.

Then Father said, "I've had about enough."

Prue slowly wiped her lips with her napkin.

"Really," she said.

"Darling," Mother placed her hand on Father's elbow.

"Leave me alone," he said. He threw his chair back and stood up. "You're to get the fuck out of my house."

"Very well," Mr. Ashton said, as he readjusted his bow tie.

"What is this all about?" Prue asked.

"Come along, dear," Mr. Ashton said, but Prue remained seated.

"Get out," Father shouted.

"If we could, we would, believe me," Prue said. "But because of the investigation—"

"You have to stay on the island, not here," Father said.

"We couldn't possibly afford—" Prue said.

"That's your problem," Father said. "You can sleep on the beach for all I care."

I have no doubt that the Ashtons would have left then if there had not been a knock at the door. Bob, the husband of the famous painter Daphne, stood outside. He wondered if we would like to watch the news on their television. A special bulletin on the kidnapping had been announced. "He could at least have told us," Father said, referring to Mr. Rossi. "Maybe he didn't know about it," Mother said. "Let's go. Come on." The Ashtons stood for a moment by the table, uncertain whether they were invited or not. Finally, they followed. However unwillingly, we were all connected by Lea's disappearance.

The room was very dark. The shutters had been closed, and the room was paneled with dark wood. The only light came from the television. The Ashtons took a seat on a long couch in one corner of the room. I could just make out the outline of their silhouettes. Prue wore a silver brooch that glinted. I sat beside Mother, while Father stood leaning against one wall. He smoked one cigarette after the next. The reception was not good and Bob kept getting up and fiddling with the antennae, apologizing. Daphne was crocheting. At one point, I thought I caught sight of someone, their son perhaps, peering through the blinds of one window.

The anchor spent a long time discoursing on the perils of waterskiing. The number of accidents had skyrocketed over the last year. Just two weeks ago, a young girl had drowned. At last, the anchor referred to the abduction of the young American girl on July 9 at the Cervo beach, one of the most popular beaches of the island, where everyone gathers because of the relative protection from the wind, although that day there had not been a breath of wind. Ironic, the anchor said. She seemed to like that word, and father made fun of her, repeating "*ironico*," each time

she used it. But there was a nervousness to his joking that suggested even at eleven to me that he did not really find it amusing. One could not help thinking of the kidnapping case earlier this summer off the Romazzino beach, in full view of everyone, the anchor continued. But in this case no one had witnessed anything. We are fortunate, however, she said, to have secured an exclusive interview with two people particularly well placed to shed light on the family and the characters involved in this tragedy: Mr. Peters, a close friend of the family's, and Signorina Dellini.

"Imagine that!" Prue said.

"Really," Father said. "I suspect that this is going to be complete waste of time."

"These reporters!" Bob said. "I'm so sorry."

"Shh," Prue said.

The first shot was of Mr. Peters standing in front of one of his paintings, a circular stairway, with a woman flying down. He wore a pale blue suit I had never seen before and the same tie had worn the evening Mr. Ashton had punched him in the face. He spoke in English and an interpreter translated. "You are close friend of the Dashleys," the anchor said.

"You could say that," Mr. Peters said. When the anchor asked him if he could shed light on the kidnapping, Mr. Peters complained of the treatment he had received at the police hands. He had been in the middle of a very important project.

"He's at last getting his moment in the limelight," Prue said

"Pathetic," Father said.

No matter what the question, Mr. Peters referred to himself

When the anchor asked him about his acquaintance with Lea, whether she had come often to see him paint, he said, "Yes, she was a great admirer of my paintings." Mr. Peters had even brought to the studio several small paintings which he insisted on producing during the interview. Asked if he had any theory about who had kidnapped Lea, Mr. Peters said, "Wish I did."

He kept repeating, "The most beautiful young girl. Just like her mother. A tragedy." The anchor said that it was her understanding that he had never been a suspect in the case. "That's right," he said.

"They arrested you for drunken behavior," she said.

"Oh, I wouldn't call it that. A bit of an overstatement," he said. "I was just having a good time. I've promised to pay back every cent. I've even offered one of my paintings as payment."

Next Mrs. Dellini, a woman I had never seen before, was interviewed. She too had obviously gone to some trouble with her attire. She wore several layers of black. A gold cross hung from her neck. The camera zeroed in on her feet, as if the cameraman had been instructed to film her new shoes, then the camera moved to her face. Her expression was dour and contrasted completely with Mr. Peters, who kept smiling. The anchor adopted a different tone. She asked if she could shed any light on the kidnapping. The old woman slowly readjusted the mantilla over her head.

She pointed a finger at the anchor. "You ought to know better than to interview someone like him." She went on to decry sensational newspapermen, the media in general. At last, the

anchor cut the woman off. They showed pictures of our villa. The anchor said that we were rumored to be immensely wealthy, related to the Aga Khan.

"The idiots," Father said, growing very excited. "Now, if they do ask us for a ransom it will be an exorbitant sum."

The program was interrupted to announce that another kidnapping had just been happily solved. A girl who had been abducted that morning had been returned unhurt to her parents that very afternoon. They showed the girl smiling with her parents, their arms around her.

Mother started to cry.

Father switched off the television. Bob and Daphne apologized profusely. They had had no idea.

We returned to the villa, single file: Father, me, Mother, Mr. Ashton, and Prue. By then the sun cast a red shadow across the sea, and the purple bougainvillea across the roof blazed. Although it was evening, it felt more like late afternoon. The tiles were still warm beneath my feet. The sea below so flat it looked like a pink lake. I remembered Lea bragging that she too could walk across the sea. I believed her until she jumped off a rock and plummeted. As she resurfaced, she laughed. In the silence I thought I heard the echo of her laughter.

No one discussed the bulletin. Everyone hurried to their respective rooms. I slept at the foot of my parents' bed.

16

There was some excitement the next day. Mr. Ashton was summoned to the police station again. Mother said she felt sorry for the Ashtons. Father said he didn't feel sorry at all. I felt completely indifferent to his plight. Then the chief of police arrived with his subaltern. He said that they needed to go through the Ashtons' room. I remember wondering if they would discover Lea's gold watch but refused to make the causal connection: The fact that I had found Lea's watch in Mr. Ashton's drawer did not mean he was guilty. I refused to envision the possibility of Mr. Ashton being involved in Lea's disappearance. All I could focus on was the heat, the feeling that it would never end. My head throbbed and I wondered if I had sunstroke again.

"I wonder what Mr. Rossi hopes to find in their room?" Mother asked.

"Who knows," Father said.

When Mr. Rossi returned from their room, he did not immediately disclose why they had found it necessary to go through their effects. Instead, he wasted time apologizing about the special broadcast. He had not been apprised of it. He thought it very unwise. But what Mrs. Dellini and Mr. Peters had divulged was not relevant to the investigation. We should be grateful for that. More troublesome were the rumors of our great fortune and relationship with the Aga Khan.

Then he said, "It might be better if the little one is not present."

Adriana stepped out of the kitchen and suggested I keep her company. She had just baked a cake and the sweet smell filled the house. But it only made me miss Lea even more. She loved sweet things and if our parents had let her she would have eaten only desserts. I was always giving her mine. Adriana was also making fresh pasta, our favorite, gnocchi, but I did not want to help her mold the dough. She even proposed to tell me a story about one of my favorite characters from the island, Eleonora d'Arborea, but I listened only to the beginning of her tale, something about a man stealing pears from a tree. I stood in the doorway.

I heard Mr. Rossi say, "Several complaints have been lodged against the Ashtons."

"What kind of complaints?" Father asked.

Mr. Rossi said that the manager of the Hotel Romazzino had lodged one for indecent behavior and nudity.

"Oh we know that manager," Father said. "Remember, he's the one who complained that Lea wasn't wearing a bikini top. If that's all—"

The telephone rang. He picked up the phone and said, "Rossi." He talked much more slowly on the phone, sarcastically at times. At last he put down the receiver. He asked Mother and Father to excuse him. He had started to say that the Ashtons had not been entirely honest about the events on the day Lea was kidnapped. A woman asserted having seen the Ashtons talking with Lea shortly before the time of her disappearance. Something they had until now denied. Apparently, between four-thirty and five, they were seen walking along the path leading from the Cervo beach to the Piccolo Pevero. The woman who saw them was terribly short-sighted. She had forgotten her glasses that day. Lea had run past the woman, stopping only when she reached the Ashtons. They had continued on and Lea had walked with them, backwards. The woman could not see her face. The woman heard only a few fragments of conversation she did not understand. Even if she had heard the whole conversation it would have made no difference because she did not know English. She did remember Lea repeating the word *why* over and over. Mrs. Ashton kept shaking her head. The woman had said *buongiorno* as she passed the Ashtons and Lea, but they had not replied. She had continued down the path, turning from time to time, to see if they were still fighting, wondering why Lea was so upset. She had seen the couple separate. Mrs. Ashton had continued on her own up the path, while Mr. Ashton had followed Lea, taking another route, a side path that led away from the sea. The woman had not come forward before because she lived in a small village and rarely read newspapers. She had heard of the kidnapping only that day.

The phone interrupted the chief of police again. He said he would be right there.

"What is it?" Mother asked.

"What did they say?" Father said.

"Have they found her?" Mother said.

"No," Mr. Rossi said. "But I must leave at once. I will let you know as soon as I know anything."

"Do you think it's possible?" Mother said to Father. "They're in some way responsible?"

"I don't know," Father said. "All I know is that they're not going to stay a minute longer."

"Why did they lie?" Mother asked.

"Maybe they were afraid," Father said. "Stupid."

"Why would they do something like that? What for?" Mother asked.

I tiptoed down the corridor to Prue's room. She was leaning over an open suitcase, which lay on their bed, her back toward me.

"How are you, my dear?" she asked. I remembered how Lea always liked being addressed as "my dear" and often imitated Prue's exact intonation. "Fine, my dear," she would say.

When I did not reply, she turned round. I stared at her feet.

"I don't know what happened to Lea," she said. "I loved her. I would never hurt her." She sat down on the bed, patting a place beside her. I sat down and continued to stare at the floor.

"You're a strange child," she said.

I knew she was thinking, "So different from Lea." I glanced at her.

"I want you to have these," she said, placing the two pillboxes, one in each palm, folding my fingers over them. "Now go. Run."

It may seem strange that I should have turned to Prue. But, in retrospect, it makes perfect sense to me. In Prue I had found an ally.

17

The next morning, the Ashtons had gone, leaving just a sprinkle of powder by their bed where Mr. Ashton must have dusted his socks. The crimson curtains had been drawn. I lay down on their bed and stared out the window at the hills that seemed to float like clouds above a thick band of mist.

The sky grew lighter but the sun never appeared. Adriana surprised me by insisting on going to the beach. The beach was deserted, just a bucket and spade abandoned in one corner. Adriana suggested I go for a swim. The sea was warm and the waves though tall were gentle. In the distance the islands were barely distinguishable from the sky. I floated for a long time inside the bay.

On the way back, Adriana told me about the charitable hostel Casa San Francesca she used to help run. She described the guests who traveled from remote areas to see their hospitalized relatives.

As we traveled along the dirt path, between the green of the golf course and the gray of the *macchia*, the sky darkened and lightning struck. Rain poured down and we hurried on, holding our towels over our heads, but then letting them drop because they were almost immediately saturated. Adriana pointed to a different path and we traveled on, traversing a burned area, where charred trees stood out against the white backdrop of the sky and the ground was black.

I see us ascending the hill to the villa, Adriana pulling me by one hand. Passing the bougainvillea I noticed how dark it looked, almost violet.

The electricity had gone out and the living room was filled with shadows. When we entered, the grown-ups did not turn. They appeared frozen, except for Father. His frame trembled but he did not cry. Mother stood at the window, the chief of police in the center of the room. Suddenly, he looked small.

Then Mother turned. "They found her."

Adriana hugged me, but I felt nothing.

I wondered how I should act. I felt that Mother and Father were waiting for me to do something, but I could not think what. I looked down at my feet. The pink sandals were black, covered with soot. I licked one finger and bent over and started to clean each plastic strip.

When I looked up, the grown-ups were in the same positions. I knew I should feel some emotion but I felt only the agony of not feeling. I walked out into the garden where it was raining. I meandered, but then I felt the urge to run as far away from the villa as I could. I was hardly aware of Adriana following me. I ran down the path Lea and I had taken our first day on the island, along the Piccolo Pevero beach, up the hill. I thought of the girl who had put herself on fire. I tried to imagine what it would feel like. First the fire flickering the soles of her feet, her legs, her stomach, her chest and then her hair. I thought I detected the smell of burned hair.

I stopped and stared down at the Cervo beach, at the narrow stretch of sand, at the gray water the exact color of the sky, and Adriana caught up with me. We stood for a long time in the rain listening to the sea roll up onto the beach and then sucked back, until I no longer felt hot but cold and at last I turned and we meandered slowly along the path.

I did not want Adriana to leave that day. She would have stayed but it was her nephew's birthday. I stood beneath the archway watching her car until it disappeared into the mist.

I remember the most innocuous details: the sound of the rain on the tiles, the hot milk with honey, the red candles we used instead of lamps that made the villa seem so different, as if we were in a dark, damp cave; even our sheets felt damp and cold to the touch. I remember finding a cardboard box with a pack of cards. Some of the cards were recognizable because they were bent. Lea and I both knew that the jack of hearts was missing one corner. The queen of spades had a crease down the middle. The summer before, we had played late every night, with our flashlights. Lea would force me to bet my allowance, my favorite doll. Her cheeks would flush as she got closer to winning. She would whistle and I would beg her to stop. Then she would jump on my bed when she had won, knocking off the dolls I had carefully lined up.

I played with my doll, taking off the green satin dress with the frill collar, noticing for the first time that the doll had been made out of a sheet. You could see the green and blue stripes. Her legs had been made uneven, the left one shorter than the right. Her arms were the same length. I twisted the doll's legs into knots, forced her to lie down then told her to stand up. "You're very naughty," I said. I made her dance. I kissed her lips.

In the morning, raindrops were reflected from the window onto the doll's face. At first I thought it was the reflection that caused her lips to look smudged but then I realized that I had smudged them myself when I had kissed the doll's lips the night before. I begged Mother to fix it. She brushed my hair with one hand. She said, "It's not the end of the world."

"But it's ruined," I said.

She wanted me to sit on her lap, but I told her I was too big. She smoothed the yellow skirt of her dress and then she said, "You must be brave, darling."

I put down the doll. I played with the cards in the box, then I stared at the painting on the wall. I would have preferred, I thought, to see Mother tear out her hair and wail, but she sat very straight in her pale yellow suit. She had pulled her hair back into a bun. She had even applied bright pink lipstick.

Mother disclosed nothing beyond the central fact. The tone of her voice annoyed me, the way she said, "You do understand, darling. She won't be coming back. You do understand, dear?" I suppose she was puzzled by my lack of response.

She stepped out into the garden and I followed her.

We circled the villa, passing from glass door to glass door, as if we were intruders. We peered into the Ashtons' room.

Despite the wind and the sand, the pink oleander had grown far into the path. Mother had to push it back in order to pass.

I kept swallowing my saliva. I wished I could throw up, but I could not. We stood just inside the curtains of her bedroom. Father lay on his stomach with one arm folded beneath him. He was snoring. The doctor had prescribed tranquilizers.

In the living room, Adriana served tea.

"Why don't you sit down," she said to Mother.

"Thank you," Mother said. She sat down but remained on the edge of her seat with her knees pressed together.

"You have Helen," Adriana said. She placed her hand on my shoulder.

"Yes," Mother said.

But she stared straight ahead at the islands in the distance. The sea was a deep blue. The white sails as if glued to its surface. She soon left the room.

"Helenina," Adriana said, "I've brought something for you I think you might like."

She produced a black case, which for an instant I took for the case of a gun. She opened the case and pulled out a violin, which she placed gently across my knees. She passed me the bow. I held the bow not knowing what to do with it.

"Thank you," I said.

"Give it to me," she said. "I can't play the way I once did, but I can at least get it in tune."

I watched her tighten the strings, play each string with her bow, then she played a short, happy tune. The sunlight danced across the wood, but I felt only sadness. I ran my hand across the blue velvet that lined the case. I waited until Adriana finished.

18

The circumstances of Lea's death came out only little by little. It's difficult for me to reconstruct the order in which I learned the details. Sometimes I no longer remember who told me what. I understand this lapse. For a time, I did not want to remember.

Father could not help going back to the incident.

"I wonder if it was an islander?" Father asked. "I really can't believe it was—"

"I don't know," Mother said.

"If it had been an islander, they would have asked for a ransom."

"Oh, what is the point, now?"

Sometimes it was not Father who brought Lea up. Sometimes it was Mother. "Why? What for? It wasn't even for money. I don't understand," she said, as she placed flowers in a vase. "If only people would stop sending flowers—"

Adriana walked over and placed her arm around Mother.

The villa had begun to look like a funeral parlor. There were vases and wreaths in every room. Hundreds of letters had arrived. A carabiniere came each day to collect the cards on the off chance that one of them might provide a clue. One morning I found a box of colored oil crayons left on the doorstep of our villa. On a tiny piece of brown wrapping paper, Mr. Peters had written, "Hi. Thought you might like these. Take care." I pictured him painting, the way he held his arm before him, squinted with one eye then the other, moved closer then away from the canvas.

The chief of police visited us from time to time. I recall one visit, in particular.

Father emerged from his room, his eyes red, his face puffy. "Still nothing?" he asked.

"I'm afraid not. A thread. Not much to go on."

The chief of police placed his hand on my shoulder.

"And how are you doing?" he asked.

"Okay," I said.

I followed him out into the garden. The sky was white. The garden enveloped in mist. The islands and the sea had disappeared. Only the golf course appeared in patches.

"When it's cloudy," I said. "All the colors disappear."

"That's right," he said, stopping so that I could catch up with him.

We meandered all the way down to the bottom of the garden where the eucalyptus trees grew. I climbed onto the stone wall that overlooked Mr. Petrinelli's garden.

Wisps of mist drifted between the pines. I thought I could hear the echo of Lea's voice saying, "You're a bore." The sky turned gray. A drop of water splashed my forehead. I could hear the sprinklers in the distance.

"It's not your fault," he said.

I was surprised that he should know this was what I was feeling, but his words brought me no comfort. He did not know the whole truth.

At this point Father emerged. His appearance was completely changed from before Lea's kidnapping. He no longer shaved. He wore his shoes without socks. He looked more like Mr. Peters.

"Can you not tell me anything more?" he asked.

Mr. Rossi shook his head.

"At least tell me where she was found. Why was the location not disclosed?" Father asked.

"We did not want people flocking to the area," Mr. Rossi said. "But I suppose I can tell you now. She was found in a nuraghe a few miles from here." He pointed in the direction of the golf course. It was still raining.

"A nuraghe," Father said.

"You know—"

"I know what it is. She always wanted—but how did she get there? Was that where—how long had—I must know. Don't you understand?" Here Father grasped Mr. Rossi's arm. Mr. Rossi whispered something in his ear. There was the sound of rain on the leaves.

Mr. Rossi opened his umbrella, holding his arm straight up in the air to protect Father. But Father seemed unaware of the attention and he stepped from beneath the umbrella, scratching his forehead on one of the ribs. He hurried up the steps.

I climbed down from the stone wall while the chief of police waited. Together we ascended the path to the villa. The rain came down hard. Already small streams had formed, flowing through the *amanti del sole*, tearing them from the ground, carrying them a short distance before abandoning them in the mud.

19

One gray day succeeded the next. The sound of water on the tiled roof was constant. Adriana came every day without fail. She would cook, tell me stories. Whereas earlier in the summer I was content to listen to any story about the island, I now insisted on stories that involved miracles or fierce retribution. My favorite miracle story was about a woman warrior, Attila Pomptila, who had been exiled with her husband, Cassio Filippo, to Bella Terra. Cassio Filippo was very ill and going to die and Attila offered her life to the gods. The gods answered her prayers, saving his life but taking hers. I liked to act out the scene with Adriana's niece, Carla. She always had to play Cassio, while I played Attila. Or I would pretend to be Eleonora d'Arborea, who punished a man for stealing pears from a tree by having his legs cut off instead of his hands.

Adriana would also tell me stories from the Bible, but she never pressed her beliefs on me. I had grown up without religion. For a short while Mother had taken us to Sunday school, but Lea and I had begged her not to because we found it boring. Father also thought it a waste of time.

How my parents came to give Lea a religious funeral I do not know. Perhaps they thought that a religious funeral would provide the sort of finality they felt was missing. Or perhaps they felt pressured by the intense religiosity of the islanders, almost exclusively Catholics, though this last seems doubtful, Father not being easy to coerce. Or perhaps Mother was responsible.

The entire island seemed to have convened for Lea's funeral. The small church, constructed of white and red stones, could not hold everyone. A crowd gathered around it. The doors were left open. It was a perfect day, much like the day Lea had disappeared. The sky was a deep blue and everything shimmered. The island was unusually green. The flowers resplendent.

The islanders were dressed in black. The women even wore crocheted black nets over their hair. The tourists, though they had made an effort to dress in black, had not all managed to. Mr. Peters arrived in the navy blue suit he had worn for his television appearance but it was already spotted with paint. He intoned loudly and out of tune, tears running down his cheeks.

The Ashtons also made an appearance. Prue wore a navy blue outfit, her husband a beige suit. They sat huddled between the islanders in the last pew. I suppose they had been requested to remain on the island. From time to time, I thought I could hear Mr. Ashton clearing his throat. Father was dressed completely in black. He towered above the islanders by at least a foot. His face was chalk colored except for a splotch of red by his ear.

Adriana, who did not need to look at the Bible because she knew the psalms by heart, kept one arm around me. I also held

Mother's hand. Every now and then she would take her hand away to wipe tears from her face.

As the ceremony progressed, the church became hotter and hotter. Women waved fans, creating a noise that sounded like rain. But when we stepped outside, the sun shone as brightly as ever. The roofs flashed in the distance. The gold handles of the coffin glinted. Father carried one corner of the coffin. He was so much taller than the islanders the coffin seemed precariously balanced. I feared that it would slip out of their hands. The graveyard was a short distance from the church, but the journey seemed very long. The congregation moved very slowly along the unpaved road. We were enveloped in dust. At the very end of the procession the chief of police followed. We had not expected him to come. His head was bowed and he looked down at his feet.

I was intensely aware of myself, aware of having to play the role of protagonist despite my intense dislike of drawing attention to myself. I felt the islanders' furtive gazes. I was grateful for Adriana's presence. I would not let go of her hand or Mother's. I pulled on their arms to and from the graveyard. My new black patent-leather shoes chafed my heels. I kept stopping to pull at the heels or to try to slide my foot farther toward the front of the shoes. At last, I took off my socks and shoes and walked barefoot.

What caught my attention were the birds that flew in the graveyard. They had pale orange, almost pink feathers. They were able to remain in one spot; they fluttered their wings, as if suspended in the air, caught in an invisible net.

The old women wailed loudly as the coffin was lowered. I stared at one old woman's hair. It looked unreal, and I wondered if it was a wig because it resembled the woolly strands left by the sheep in the pastures. The crowd of people advanced slowly, while sheep grazed unhurriedly. Lambs bleated, calling back and forth to one another. The bleats were at different pitches, some low and some high and some sounding like groans. I remembered Lea imitating their bleats, how we laughed when the sheep had responded to her.

At the villa, Mother tucked me into my bed, then sat by my side and held my hand. "We have to believe," she said, as much to herself as to me. I kept visualizing the last time I had seen Lea, the sun on her hair, the way she had skipped, the shadow that flickered beside her.

The feelings I had were echoed in the grown-ups. Occasionally, someone would start to voice a regret. I recall Mother saying, "And to think I wasn't concerned when she disappeared at the beach!" Father would hasten to reassure her, perhaps fearing that if we all confessed it would be too much to bear.

Father was almost never at home. He scoured the island in his Jeep as if he could still find Lea, returning with his hair stiff with dust, his face red from the heat. Mother became more considerate of me, as if trying to make up for her failure with Lea. But this was almost worse than Father's rejection. On several occasions she offered to buy me a blackboard, something I had been begging for for months, but was no longer interested in. I filled my time pasting into a notebook religious pictures I had cut out of magazines Adriana had brought me. I admired the pictures of saints, the pink and gold colors. But I did not believe in God.

It was Mother who embraced religion. She started going to church every morning. She carried a Bible and a rosary. She said that if it weren't for me, she would join a convent. She was going to convert to Catholicism.

And for once Mother and Father were in agreement over something: the necessity of commemorating Lea's death. They planned an immense mausoleum of pink marble, which dwarfed all the other tombs in the cemetery.

One day, returning from a walk with Adriana, I found Lea's glasses on my bedside table. For a moment, I felt elated—Lea had come back. But then I realized that Adriana had simply found Lea's glasses and thought they were mine. Even after all these years, I keep them in my bedside drawer. The glasses no longer look oversized, but they bring back the image of Lea's face, pressed against the dirty cab window our first day of the last summer on the island.

20

We lingered on the island, I suspect, because my parents were reluctant to leave the scene of Lea's disappearance. To do so would mean acknowledging that a chapter was closed, or perhaps it was the opposite, they lingered in the hopes of a further finality. They hoped that the investigation would lead to the capture of the perpetrator.

The details from the case were kept from me. I am sure my parents thought there was no point in disclosing facts that could only upset me further. Adriana kept every article in an album very similar to the one she had collected before. She told me that she was keeping it until I was of age.

We stayed on the island through August into mid-September. By then most of the tourists had gone; even Mr. Peters was rumored to have returned to the United States. The funeral home director was the only person who remained. Every afternoon he would leave on our doorstep a copy of the International Herald Tribune, but father left the papers where they had been dropped, and after a few weeks, he stopped coming. So few events punctuated our day that I found myself missing even his brief visits. I liked to watch from the window of the kitchen the huge black hearse stop in the archway of our villa, the way he would trip halfway down the alley, before flinging the newspaper onto our doorstep, turning abruptly on his heel.

The area surrounding our villa was now deserted, the houses closed until the following summer. At night, we no longer heard the sound of people's voices, laughter, drift from neighboring villas. It seemed particularly dark without the lights from nearby houses. Even the wind refused our company. Father no longer stepped outside the villa. He forbade anyone to enter or leave. He would not let Adriana's husband, Michelino, tend the garden. "What do I care? It can all go to rack and ruin!" he said. Only Mother and Adriana broke his edict; Adriana to spend time with me and prepare our meals, Mother to make her daily excursions to a nearby church.

I would not have been surprised to continue in this way forever. But one morning Father abruptly announced that we were going home. We packed our bags hastily, abandoning anything that could not be placed in our valises.

Sometimes, I picture the villa's gradual deterioration, weeks, months after we left; the crumbs on our leftover dishes, a trail of ants going from the floor to the table. The fine ocher dust covering the blue furniture, and eventually sand seeping in, sparkling like tiny diamonds against the red tiled floor. Perhaps even a gecko. We could not have taken most of the furniture had we wanted to since it was immovable, carved out of the stone of the island.

Then I remind myself that Adriana would not have let this happen. Perhaps she had found room in her apartment for the mother-of-pearl light fixtures, the glass lamps filled with tiny pink shells, the sheets Father had bought in Genoa and the bedspreads that matched the curtains. It pleased me to imagine our things tucked amongst her possessions.

The morning of our departure, Michelino drove us in the big Jeep to the airport. I sat up front, squeezed between him and Adriana. I knew that this would be the last time I would see Bella Terra. I remember feeling very high in the Jeep. I felt I could see more. Noticing in the distance a particularly tall mountain, I wondered if it was the same mountain a shepherd climbed in search of an eaglet, tumbling to his death. Adriana had told me that the islanders believed that the souls of the damned were reunited in its crevice.

Father said, "Imagine what the island must have been like centuries ago, before foreigners invaded it."

I pictured the island at its conception, surging from the ocean, 450 million years before. I imagined it lush with trees. I could not believe that we were leaving Lea behind. She was not in the enormous pink marble tomb Mother and Father had chosen to bury her in. I preferred to imagine that she was in the pellucid water and the azure sky. I was glad that, before leaving the villa, I had hastily written her name on the blank granite where the name of our villa would never be inscribed.

As Adriana said good-bye to me, lifting me up with both arms so that my feet no longer touched the ground, she whispered that she was pregnant again. She would keep in touch. Eight months later, I received a birth announcement. A little girl, Paola, had been born, seven pounds and eight ounces.

Over the years, Adriana kept in touch by sending me photographs of Paola, marking important moments: her christening, her first day of school, her confirmation. By the time she sent me the album chronicling the events of that summer, I was seventeen, and I wanted nothing more than to forget. I might never have looked into it again if Adriana had not sent me a newspaper clipping that included a photograph.

I recognized Mr. Ashton's face immediately. The black hair, greased down and parted to one side. The only difference were the lines across his forehead and around his eyes. Most unusual in these cases, he had finally been apprehended. Mr. and Mrs. Ashton had been staying at the Hotel del Sol in Corsica. He had confessed to molesting several girls but denied "hurting" any. However, when I reviewed Adriana's album, articles revealed Lea had been strangled, ashes found in her hair. There was no doubt in my mind that he was guilty.

From the information released and my own secret knowledge, I formed a picture of what happened to Lea. At first the picture was out of focus, but gradually it grew sharper.

She walks through Mr. Petrinelli's garden, the white of her dress catching the sunlight, contrasting with the green of the pines. Resin glistens along the seams of the trees. She stops to inhale the scent and sit down in its shade. She plucks dead pine needles from the ground, then lets them drop as if they were sand. From time to time, she glances back at the path, white in the sun. She pictures Prue wearing her silk robe with the dragon which is gold on the outside but purple on the inside. She thinks she hears Prue call her name. Hearing a rustle of leaves, she turns, but it is only a brown bird which flutters and drops out of sight. The tops of the bushes waver but there is not a breath of wind. The heat creates the illusion of movement.

Gradually, the sun shifts and at last it is clearly closer to four than to three. She does not need to glance at her watch to know. She has always been able to tell time without a watch. She runs down the hill, past the hibiscuses, skirting the golf course. She races across the Piccolo Pevero beach, along that stretch of sand where yellow nettles grow, and then she climbs the hill. She does not notice a woman standing to one side. In the distance, she sees the Ashtons. They saunter arm over arm. She waits until they reach her. She stands in their path, on the swath of wild grass that cuts the road in two. "Why didn't you come?" she asks Prue.

"Where?" Prue asks.

"Why?" she asks.

"I don't understand," Prue says. "Where was I—"

"I—" she says.

"What does it matter?" Prue says. "Here I am now." She reaches out as if to draw Lea to her.

But Lea runs down a side path, her eyes squinting in the glare of the sun. The light glances off the brown bushes with their hard leaves and though it's past four it feels as if it's noon. Heat rises from the ground. She stops only when she gets out of breath. In the distance she can see the yellow tops of the white golf carts, the golf course, kept green, despite the wind and the sand.

She stops to extract a burr from the hem of her dress, which pricks her knee. Her legs have been scratched, but she doesn't remember feeling any pain. Hearing a noise, she turns, thinking it's Prue, but it's him. Mr. Ashton. He's wearing white shorts and a white tennis

shirt, leather shoes. Just before he reaches her, she lets the skirt of her
dress drop. She cannot get the burr out. She hurries on. "Where are
you running off to?" he calls out. She says, "Home," but she slows
down because she doesn't want him to think that she's in that much
of a hurry.

"Would you like to see a nuraghe? Do you know what they are?"
"Of course," she says. She covers her eyes with one hand.
"It's not far," he says. "It's really on the way home."
"How far?"
"Not very far."

His white tennis shirt is buttoned to the neck. It looks too tight.
He turns down a narrow lane. She follows him. He shuffles fast.
She notices patches of light thrown onto one of the dark brown bushes
which litter the path. The scent of myrtle is very strong. From time to
time, she stops to detach more burrs from her dress. "Are we almost
there?" she asks, glancing back at the beach and the brilliant
turquoise water. The sun reflects off the water and somehow the
dazzling light is reassuring. She can make out the beach umbrellas.
But she wishes she had brought her hat or at least her sunglasses. She
can't remember where she left them. She thinks of turning back, of
making up some excuse. But Mr. Ashton slows down. He asks her
what she wants to be when she grows up. She tells him that she
doesn't have a clue. She shrugs. "You're different from your sister,"
he says. "I guess," she says. He talks fast as he walks and sometimes
she catches only a few words. His words get swallowed up by his
chin. But he doesn't seem to expect an answer. He reaches inside his
back pocket but his hand comes out empty. He forgets to push the
inside of his pocket back in so it hangs out.

At last, around a bend, they come up on a nuraghe. It's identical to the one she saw by the road the first day on the island, a huge cone-shaped stone with a blunt top. Only it's less impressive close up; it seems smaller and half broken. "Why don't you come see it from the other side?" he says. She follows him through the long grass, wondering if it's true that there are no snakes on the island. She doesn't mind snakes. But it's the kind of thing Helen would worry about. The other side of the nuraghe is no more interesting. There's a gash in the wall and wild white flowers grow along the sides. He disappears inside a narrow opening. She takes a step forward, then stands with one foot inside the nuraghe, the other outside, hesitating. He grabs her by the shoulder and pulls her in. Her arm gets scraped. "Careful," she says. He holds her against his chest, his arms tightly wrapped around her. She strains against him, kicks his shins, but his grasp is so tight she can barely breathe. "Moron," she says. She cannot believe that he is doing this. Mr. Ashton. Prue's husband. She goes limp. She can feel his breath on her hair, smell the scent of his cigar. "Are you going to be good?" he asks. Sunlight filters through an opening in the ceiling. She can see the sky. A perfect blue. He lets go of her, tells her to take off her clothes. "No way," she says, and crosses her arms over her chest. "You're crazy." She opens her mouth to scream again, but he throws himself onto her, knocking her to the ground. She has no breath: it feels just like when she fell off a horse once onto her back. He's lying on top of her. She closes her eyes. She cannot breathe. She feels him get up and she opens her eyes. He looks down and says, "I'll strangle you if you scream again." She feels faint, tries to pull the skirt of her dress over her knees. He opens the zipper to his shorts. He moves his hand up

182

and down. He seems to grow desperate. "Take off your dress," he says. She screams and screams but there is no one to hear her. He kneels beside her. His hands seize her neck. His fingers tighten. His face fades against the dark. Something hits her head. The taste of blood is in her mouth. She can feel him standing looking down at her. He slides something off her wrist. The watch her father gave her. She feels the urge to stop him to grab it back but her arm remains still. A streak of light warms one side of her face. She pictures her family: Helen, Mum and Dad. They stand against the macchia. *The sky has turned pink and the sea is tinged gold. The tops of the bushes glow. As if on fire.*

ACKNOWLEDGMENTS

Many thanks to my mother and father, ardent supporters of my work. I would also like to thank my best readers: my sister, Cybele, who read countless drafts, Julie Abbruscato, Andrew Zeller, Tess Callahan James, and Nicole Bokat. Many thanks to my extraordinary agent, Anne Edelstein, and her wonderful assistant Emilie Stewart; my indefatigable editor, Jeanne McCulloch, without whom this book would not be what it is, and her superb assistants, Michelle Wildgen and Meg Storey; and last, but not least, my husband, Kevin.

A NOTE ON THE AUTHOR

Sasha Troyan is the author of *Angels in the Morning* (Permanent Press). She lives in Montclair, New Jersey, with her husband and two sons.

A NOTE ON THE TYPE

The text of this book is set in Linotype Janson. The original types were cut in about 1690 by Nicholas Kis, a Hungarian working in Amsterdam. The face was misnamed after Anton Janson, a Dutchman who worked at the Ehrhardt Foundry in Leipzig, where the original Kis types were kept in the early eighteenth century. Monotype Ehrhardt is based on Janson. The original matrices survived in Germany and were acquired in 1919 by the Stempel Foundry. Hermann Zapf used these originals to redesign some of the weights and sizes for Stempel. This Linotype version was designed to follow the original types under the direction of C. H. Griffith.